D1152890

A. V. Denham taught in both London and Hong Kong before moving to Wales with her family. After joining the Women's Royal Voluntary Service, she later trained for the emergency services. Denham enjoys travelling, gardening, and is also interested in goldwork. She lives in Monmouth.

# THE GIRL WHO DISAPPEARED

Fifty-one-year-old Hetty is an unmarried schoolteacher who has lived with her mother all her life. On her mother's death she is liberated and finds herself wooed by Clive and the widowed artist Tom, father of one of her students, Megan. Megan's friends, Jit and Balbiro, are Sikh cousins who are facing arranged marriages. While Jit agrees and accepts her fate, Balbiro rebels against her family's choice and disappears. But, as Hetty and Jit both learn to manipulate events to their own advantage, the true horror of Balbiro's situation is revealed.

A. V. DENHAM

# THE GIRL WHO DISAPPEARED

Complete and Unabridged

# ULVERSCROFT
## Leicester

First published in Great Britain in 2006 by
Robert Hale Limited
London

First Large Print Edition
published 2007
by arrangement with
Robert Hale Limited
London

The moral right of the author has been asserted

British Library CIP Data

Denham, A. V. (Angela Veronica), *1936 –*
The girl who disappeared.—Large print ed.—
Ulverscroft large print series: general fiction
1. Sikh women—Social conditions—Fiction
2. Forced marriage—Fiction 3. Missing persons—
Fiction 4. Large type books
I. Title
823.9'14 [F]

ISBN 978–1–84617–704–0

Published by
F. A. Thorpe (Publishing)
Anstey, Leicestershire

Set by Words & Graphics Ltd.
Anstey, Leicestershire
Printed and bound in Great Britain by
T. J. International Ltd., Padstow, Cornwall

This book is printed on acid-free paper

# 1

The picture had been sold.

Hetty's heart gave a lurch of disappointment. The picture had been the only exhibit in the window of the gallery for over a week. It was a small watercolour of the Blorange in a gilt frame. Now a large stone otter occupied pride of place. Hetty Loveridge, in Otterhaven's Church Street to shop for the weekend, had just turned away despondently when out of the corner of her eye she saw the easel standing on the floor of the gallery, obscured by the sculpture. The watercolour still stood on it.

Go on, urged the devil of extravagance inside her. It won't do any harm just to look. The circular path round the Blorange, one of the mountains that loomed over Abergavenny, was one of Hetty's favourite walks: a walk that was not too isolated but with far-reaching views on clear days.

Hetty put down her heavy bags thankfully and peered through the glass. Why not go inside? said the voice in her head. You'd get a better view close up.

'I'm not going to buy it,' she said aloud.

'That's a shame,' a voice, a man's voice with a hint of amusement in it, came from somewhere over her right shoulder. 'Were you hankering after the otter? Splendid creature. It's had a lot of interest, I understand. I wouldn't mind having it in my garden.'

'The otter?' Hetty smiled uncertainly, flustered by being caught talking to herself. 'You'd need a large garden to do that justice. No, I was looking at the painting on the easel.'

'Were you? Why don't you go inside and take a closer look?'

'Because I should probably fall in love with it and I can't afford it,' she admitted frankly.

'There's no charge for browsing. That's what galleries are for.'

This time Hetty laughed. 'Are you trying to tempt me?'

The man merely inclined his head, opened the gallery door and held it for her.

Her response had sounded so arch, almost as though she was flirting! Mortified by her reaction both to the man and the situation, Hetty nevertheless found herself picking up her shopping bags and following him. But once inside, the man disappeared through a door near some stairs at the back of the gallery. Hetty supposed he was a friend of

Vera, the gallery's owner. No wonder he'd enticed her in.

Her equanimity somewhat restored, Hetty said good morning to Vera, who was sitting behind a desk mending a frame.

'Lovely morning,' said Vera cheerfully. 'Looking for anything special or are you just looking?'

'Just looking, thank you,' replied Hetty carefully. She put down the shopping bags by the desk and turned to the painting.

Vera eyed her narrowly. 'How's your mother?'

'Quite well, thank you.'

'Splendid woman, for her age. So elegant and keeps herself so busy. You'd never know she was — '

'Not that old,' said Hetty hastily.

'No, of course not. She does a lot for the church, doesn't she?'

'Mother goes to church regularly,' Hetty agreed, adding wryly, 'far more frequently than I do.'

'Can't say I have the inclination for it myself, either.'

'I walk most Sundays,' offered Hetty. 'There's such beautiful countryside around Otterhaven.'

'Like in the picture,' suggested Vera meaningfully.

'Just so.' Hetty was not to be dragooned, turning first to the stone otter, finding it impossible to resist stroking the creature's smooth back.

'Funny how everyone does that.'

'Does what?'

'Stroke the otter.'

'Do they? It is a lovely piece. But far too big for our garden.'

'The picture is a good size for a small space.'

'I suppose it is.' Defeated, Hetty turned towards the picture she had come into the gallery to examine.

The artist had captured the mountain in autumn: the leaves on the deciduous trees had turned and were a riot of glorious colour, from the yellow gold of the larch to the reddish orange of the beeches interspersed with pointed evergreens. Above the tree line dead bracken glowed burnt sienna. Clouds scudded across a blue sky and you could sense the dying year, feel the cold. There was the bowl where, hidden from the valley, there was that magical tree-ringed pool, the rocks at the summit, grey granite. In her mind's eye Hetty traced the different routes she took depending on her whim. The artist had also included the mast which was just above Foxhunter's Grave. Hetty often sat on the stone seat beside this grave to eat an apple before finishing her walk.

It was exquisite, delicately executed, lovingly tinted. Hetty so admired the skill that could produce a work of art that appeared effortless. Her mother had a collection of local Otterhaven prints which she and her husband, Hetty's long-dead father, had acquired but paintings, whether in oil or watercolour, did not appeal to Mrs Loveridge. Hetty glanced at the price tag and her eyes widened. She checked the tiny signature: *T. Gillard.* That explained it. Tom Gillard was a watercolourist with a growing reputation, both locally and in Cardiff — possibly further afield, for all she knew. His daughter, Megan, had been a weekly boarder at the school where Hetty taught, an independent day school for girls, and one of Tom Gillard's views of Gaer Hill adorned a wall in the head's study. She turned away. She wanted that painting badly but if she bought it there was no way she could afford her summer holiday in Scotland, a decent wedding present for her goddaughter and re-cover the davenport in her bedroom, which was sadly shabby.

You need to sort your priorities, woman, came that inner voice again. Wedding present, of course, and the holiday because you need that and you've promised your godmother to visit her, but why not just buy a throw for the davenport?

'Mother abhors throws.'

'I beg your pardon. Did you say something, Hetty?'

'I'm sorry, Vera. I must have been talking to myself. I seem to be doing a lot of that recently.'

'You know they say it's because you get sensible answers.'

Vera smiled at Hetty and for the first time Hetty responded genuinely; two women of a certain age aware that they were sufficiently comfortable with themselves to indulge in small eccentricities they would have scorned a decade before.

'I'll take that,' Hetty said, on impulse.

'Really? I've watched you look at it through the window several times but I never thought you'd actually buy it. Tom'll be pleased,' Vera said, carefully taking down the painting from the easel.

'Why will I be pleased?' asked the man from the street, emerging from the back office.

'Your painting of the Blorange has gone. Hetty's just bought it. You'll have to bring in something else now.'

'How kind of you, Mrs . . . ?'

'Haven't you two met? I assumed you knew each other when you came in together. Hetty, this is Tom Gillard, the artist. Tom, meet Hetty Loveridge.'

'I don't usually go in for impulse buys but I couldn't resist this,' Hetty said ruefully. 'I suppose that's why I hadn't come in before.'

'Do you know the Blorange area?'

'I've lived in Otterhaven for years, Mr Gillard . . . '

'Tom.'

She ignored that. 'And I walk on the Blorange and in the Black Mountains when the weather is good.'

'Then I hope you get years of pleasure from it.' He turned away, to busy himself with a letter which was addressed to him at the gallery.

She scarcely bothered to sigh at the curtailment of their exchange. Men did not linger to converse with her; had not done so for as long as she could remember. Hetty did not believe that her manner was particularly off-putting, nor was it that she was repellent to look at. Aged fifty-one, Hetty might be of mere medium height with a frame that veered to the solid rather than the svelte, but her dark blonde hair (which as yet she had not thought needed tinting) was cut short by a young woman who knew exactly how to style

7

it and her dark blue eyes were large and still thickly lashed. She was also blessed with excellent vision which meant that those eyes were not concealed behind lenses or unflattering frames.

What Hetty was dimly aware of without exactly knowing how to cope with it or why this was so, was that there seemed to be an aura surrounding her that acted as effectively as a solid barrier between herself and anyone she had not known for many years.

Covertly she gazed at Tom Gillard while her painting was being wrapped. She saw a man of about her own age, possibly a year or so older since his hair was liberally peppered with grey and his face was craggy with lines that confirmed a life well lived. His demeanour was confident, self-assured, that of a man who wore his years lightly. Casually dressed in a well-cut cord jacket with neatly pressed twill trousers, a dark green polo shirt and polished brown leather shoes, he was not in the least artistic — whatever that might mean.

'Hi, Dad. Sorry I'm late. Saw this amazing top in — Hello, Miss Loveridge. Wow, you're not actually buying one of his pictures, are you?' The gallery door had been flung open and before she was half inside a rush of exclamations was pouring from Megan

Gillard, a tall, jeans-clad girl, a striking teenager with a mass of glossy black hair which today she wore loose, trailing way below her shoulders.

'Megan . . . '

'I'm not being impertinent, Dad. I think it's great. I mean, I think it's great you've sold a picture and I'm glad Miss Loveridge has bought it. Now you'll have something to remember me by,' she ended with the brashness of youth that sets itself at the centre of its own universe.

'Miss Loveridge . . . '

'Hetty,' murmured Hetty, belatedly.

'Miss Loveridge, now I realize who you are. I thought the name was familiar. Delighted to meet you at last.' Tom Gillard, his manner subtly altered, held out his hand, which Hetty shook, finding his clasp warm and firm. 'If it hadn't been for you and the book club this girl of mine wouldn't have opened a work of fiction during the past two years.'

'I think that's a bit of an exaggeration,' objected Hetty, taking the proffered PIN machine from Vera. 'There. That's done.'

'And it's not true, Dad. I love reading.'

'Proper books, I was talking about, not just slushy novels.'

'The whole concept of the book club is to introduce all kinds of books, fiction and non-fiction, modern novels and — '

'I know all about Shakespeare and Dickens — '

'From films and DVDs,' interrupted her father in his turn.

'You'd be surprised how many girls read the book after watching the film,' said Hetty.

'I certainly would,' replied Tom Gillard drily.

'Why don't you come and have a coffee with us,' suggested Megan disarmingly, 'then we can talk about the book club in comfort. Besides, I didn't get any breakfast.'

'More fool you,' said her father. 'That would be a good idea, Miss Loveridge, only we have an appointment with the bank. I'm so sorry. I'd have liked to continue this conversation.'

'And I must get all this home, as well as my painting,' said Hetty. 'It's just as well I've not far to go.'

'Do you live in Otterhaven?'

'Just round the corner.'

'We really can't have coffee now, but I think I owe you at least a drink for putting up with Megan all this time. Could we meet later on?'

'Oh,' said Hetty. 'Why, yes. Yes, I'd like that.'

'Excellent. What about The Otter. Say,

6.30? I'll meet you in the small lounge to the left of the bar.' Tom Gillard nodded towards Vera, a silent but avid listener, put his hand firmly on his daughter's shoulder and guided her in the direction of the door.

Hetty watched father and daughter leave the gallery, quite bemused by the turn of events. She could scarcely remember the last time a man had invited her to anything remotely social. Though by no means pretentious, The Otter was an ivy-clad old hostelry, scarcely modernized, with a solid reputation for comfort in its small, dark reception rooms and large, comfortable chairs into which its clientele could sink after a hard day's work and enjoy a variety of drinks including real ale for which people would come from miles around.

'Well,' said Vera, sounding complacent, 'that's a good morning's work.'

'What do you mean?'

'He's quite a catch. But though he's a widower, he does have a bit of a reputation, you know.'

'I don't,' said Hetty, her tone of voice suggesting that she wouldn't believe it anyway.

'Gets through women in droves. They say,' Vera added hastily, seeing the glacial look on Hetty's face. 'But I wouldn't like you to be

11

under any misapprehension.'

'Vera, the man's only asked me to have a drink with him. I know Megan from the book club. I've just bought one of his paintings.'

'Quite.'

Hetty left the gallery. If she'd been younger the word 'flounced' might have applied, but she rolled her eyes instead. Stupid woman. She'd known Vera for many years, though they'd never been particularly close friends. Now she knew why.

No one could have said why it was that Hetty Loveridge had never married. There had been an attachment at university and a holiday fling in Florence with a romantic Italian when she was thirty, but distance had cooled the first and the inevitability of irreconcilable disparity of character the second. Soon afterwards Hetty accepted her single status with the same equanimity she acknowledged her mother's supremacy in her life. The menopause came early. At forty-five there were six uncomfortable months of hot flushes and shortness of temper. HRT followed, but a year later Hetty discontinued the treatment and (somewhat to her doctor's surprise) found the original symptoms had disappeared. Without using the word spinster, which had connotations of dried-up crabbiness, Hetty had long-since accepted that she was middle-aged and would be so until she retired, at which point, presumably, she would join the ranks of the elderly.

The thought that an acquaintance, especially one of long-standing, might consider her interested in men — for whatever purpose — was one that disconcerted her.

Still, it had been quite a morning's work, buying a painting and meeting Tom Gillard. She was actually looking forward to the evening.

★ ★ ★

Laura Blackstone was hovering by the Loveridges' front door as Hetty reached it. Hetty and her mother lived in a small cottage, part of a terrace of assorted cottages with tiny gardens at the back, in a quiet street not far from the centre of Otterhaven.

'Good morning. How are you?' Hetty said brightly. 'I thought you were playing bridge with Mother until lunchtime.'

'So did I,' Laura Blackstone replied. 'But your mother hasn't turned up and it's not like Joan to forget a bridge session.'

'No, it isn't,' agreed Hetty, carefully leaning the painting against the wall. 'Have you rung the bell?'

'I've been doing that for several minutes.'

'Let me open the door.'

Hetty turned the key and held the door open so that Mrs Blackstone might precede her. 'Do go in.'

'Good gracious! Joan . . . '

★   ★   ★

*'For a thousand years in thy sight are but as yesterday . . . O teach us to number our days: that we may apply our hearts unto wisdom . . . '*

Hetty Loveridge fixed her dry eyes on the modest wreath of lilies adorning her mother's uncompromisingly plain coffin that stood in mute reproach in the nave of the parish church of Otterhaven, and contemplated her future.

It was the following Wednesday, an afternoon in July and the start of the summer holidays. So typical of Joan Loveridge to have made a clean break with her own life at a time most inconvenient for her daughter, the end of the school year with the formalities of Hetty's work as head of department barely completed. Moreover it was a week before her fortnight break in Scotland. Too short a time in which to cope with not only the red tape but the general messiness of death. Joan would have abhorred the messiness; would have denied that it could possibly exist. But it did.

Hetty sighed and dragged her mind back to the ritual as laid down by the Book of Common Prayer in the time of King Edward VI. *'Death is swallowed up in victory. O death, where is thy sting?'* None of the newfangled modern rites for Joan, who frequently expressed contempt for what she called the dumbing down of the Anglican ritual. Hetty, who had some sympathy for her mother's point of view in this, had a sneaking suspicion that Joan would have preferred everything still to have been in Latin. (She had been shocked when Roman Catholics had been abjured by the Second Vatican Council in 1962 to revert to the vernacular.)

There was to be no open grave but a cremation. Some years previously Joan had written down the instructions for this very service, choosing the hymns and the readings, which were in the same envelope as her will. Many years ago when her husband, Hetty's father, died unexpectedly Joan had chosen the spot overlooking the river in the graveyard where their ashes were to be buried side by side. Not fearing her own death (though she probably thought it was years away), Joan had also made sure that Hetty understood exactly what her wishes were. *'I want a plain coffin,*

15

mind, and a simple box for the ashes. Don't you waste my money on anything fancy that'll be going up in smoke.' Then, neither of them had expected Joan to succumb to a massive, and totally unexpected, coronary at the age of seventy-six, when she was apparently in robust health and spirits, putting on her tailored jacket in the sitting-room before walking down the road to play bridge.

The green-suited ambulance driver, a slim young woman, and her equally slight male partner, called by Laura Blackstone after she and Hetty had discovered Joan on the floor, had not even had the inconvenience of bringing the body down the narrow and steep town cottage stairs. Both had tried resuscitation (though it was plain to Laura that Joan had died long before they had arrived) before whisking their patient off to Nevill Hall Hospital where DOA, dead on arrival, was pronounced. This had involved a post mortem, but the cause of death was a massive heart attack. Joan could have gone at any time in the past five years — or she could have survived until she was well into her eighties.

What will I do without her? Hetty asked herself, as she stood at the lych gate shaking hands with the small congregation of a dozen or so elderly women, half a dozen even older

16

men and, to her surprised pleasure, three of her own colleagues.

Never in her life — except for those terms when she was at university — had Hetty lived apart from her mother for anything more than a week or so. Joan had been the centre of that life, her mentor, the mainstay of her existence, latterly her responsibility even though that responsibility had been worn lightly. Hetty might have brought into the household from her salary rather more than was her mother's pension, might have been the one who sorted the bills, but it was still Joan who insisted on writing the cheques (so much easier to do things by direct debit). Now change was upon her.

'What will we do without Joan on the flower rota?' A powdery kiss was bestowed on Hetty's cheek. 'I suppose you wouldn't . . . No, no, of course not. Joan always said you had no eye for line.'

'It's more a case of no time, I'm afraid.' Hetty tried to sound apologetic. She was certainly not going to inherit her mother's church duties, any more than she was intending to fill Joan's seat at the bridge table. Hetty loathed the whole rigmarole of bridge: whose week it was to set up the table and provide the sherry and nibbles, the ritual of dressing for it, the resulting snippets of gossip (some of it surprisingly perspicacious). Instead Hetty insisted she could hardly tell a club from a spade and was totally unable to master the intricacies of trumping.

'There's always the school holidays. No. Never mind. Flower arranging is a skill not given to everyone.'

'Such a loss.' Hetty's hand was pressed limply.

'You won't be thinking of selling, I suppose?'

How insensitive even the oldest friends could be, was Hetty's thought, much later, when it was all over: the ragged hymn singing as the curtains slowly closed round the coffin in the crematorium, which was surrounded by stately trees, its beautiful setting the Royal Forest of Dean; the desultory conversation over ham, egg and cress, and cheese and tomato sandwiches, tea, sherry and small cakes back at the house. (Her mother's generation never offered wine at funerals.) Scarcely waiting for Joan to be cold before they were wondering if they might buy her cottage, so conveniently situated for Otter-haven's small row of shops. Where did they think Joan's daughter would go — Cardiff or London?

For the first time in her life she was truly alone. Hetty swallowed a lump in her throat.

18

She was not going to weep. There was far too much washing up to do. Suppressing a sigh, she began to gather up the cups and saucers. She'd used the best china and the silver teaspoons. Joan would have expected no less. '*I suppose you'll let your standards slip when I'm gone.*' She could hear her mother as plainly as if she were in the room. Well, Hetty might, or she might not. But at any rate either way, it was entirely up to her.

★ ★ ★

Two days later, a dull day with a menacing sky, Hetty Loveridge came face to face with Tom Gillard in the butcher's. Otterhaven was one of those few remaining largish villages fortunate enough to have retained in its street of small shops the old-fashioned useful ones: butcher, baker, general store, wool shop, dress shop and second-hand bookshop. In the butcher's it appeared Tom had just paid for a chicken. Hetty had come for a lamb chop.

'Miss Loveridge.' His face was impassive as he acknowledged her, his tone clipped. There was a token nod of his head.

Hetty had the distinct impression that only innate good manners had prevented him from looking through her, though instinctively she had smiled at him. She found it puzzling, but since her mother's death Hetty had found so much that was confusing to deal with that the apparent incivility of an acquaintance was not important. Almost immediately she forgave him; already she had discovered that there were a number of people (some of whom she had regarded as friends) who by a quirk of personality were not able to discuss death. These often found some pressing reason to cross the street in order not to have to press her hand or mention her mother. No doubt Tom Gillard was one such.

'Mr Gillard . . . ' Hetty's smile froze on the instant and her greeting emerged uncertainly. For only then had she remembered their last encounter and how he had invited her to meet him for a drink at The Otter. It had been the day of her mother's death. Hetty had entirely forgotten their date — if that description could be given to such a minor social arrangement. *Of course* she had forgotten their date. 'Mr Gillard . . . ' she repeated, her tone more positive. But it was too late. The door had closed behind him.

'A lamb chop,' she said mechanically, when the shopkeeper had asked her twice for her order. 'A small one,' she added, her heart sinking, seeing in the man's face recollection of all those times the Loveridges had bought two lamb chops, two of everything. The larger portion had always been eaten by Joan, who loved red meat.

*Damn, damn.* If only she had thought to phone him. How extraordinarily ill-mannered Tom Gillard must think her. Hetty wondered if it would be a good idea to buy a small card and send it to him with a note of apology. She hated the thought that anyone should think that she was lacking in social graces, particularly Tom Gillard.

Then common sense came to her rescue. Why on earth, she wondered, should it matter that he thought her so crass? She would do no such thing as to write to him. So humiliating it would appear, as though she were begging for sympathy — worse, for a repeat invitation. Hetty sighed. She would just have to live with the knowledge that she was not one of Tom Gillard's favourite people. After all, they were hardly likely to meet in the general course of things, as they had never met before *that* day. And now that Megan had left school there was even less likelihood that they would meet again.

He would have completed his purchases, be on his way home by now, so it was unlikely they would bump into each other again. But to make absolutely sure, Hetty decided that she would leave the toothpaste, her last errand at the general store, for another time and go straight home. After all, there was plenty for her to do there as she had yet to sort out the cloakroom cupboard with its quota of her mother's outdoor clothes. She would do that, Hetty determined, fill a bag for the inevitable charity shop (which had taken the place of a very useful old-fashioned hardware store when its owners retired), and once she had delivered the bag in the afternoon she would buy the toothpaste.

# 2

To Hetty's dismay, outside the butcher's shop both Tom and Megan Gillard were arguing heatedly, blocking the pavement so that she had to step into the road to pass them.

'No, you may not go to Jit's uninvited,' declared Tom.

'Dad. You know Jit's parents are always glad to see me.'

'It might be inconvenient this time, and as you've not been able to phone her, how do you know you'll be welcome?'

'I just do,' the girl answered sulkily.

A car swooshed by, its wheels sending a spray of cold and dirty water from a puddle over Hetty's ankles. She gasped.

'Bloody drivers!' exclaimed Tom. 'Are you all . . . Ah, Miss Loveridge,' he said, his voice noticeably colder.

'Did you get very wet?' asked Megan.

'I shall survive,' answered Hetty stoically, shaking cold and dirty water from her red moccasins. 'Some drivers can be so inconsiderate.'

'Miss Loveridge, I was so sorry to hear about your mother.' Megan's words of sympathy were accompanied by a warm smile.

'Thank you. It was sadly unexpected.'

Tom Gillard frowned. 'Have I missed something here?'

'Miss Loveridge's mother died just over a week ago, Dad. It was in the local paper. I told you.'

'Did you?'

'There, you weren't listening, as usual.'

'Megan . . . Please accept my sympathies, too, Miss Loveridge. Even if you are expecting it, the death of a parent is a dreadful wrench.'

'Mr Gillard,' said Hetty in a rush, 'it happened the day I bought your painting. When I arrived home I found her on the floor. My mother, that is. She died suddenly. That was the reason I never went to The Otter. I'm afraid I forgot all about it until I saw you this morning. You must think me quite terribly impolite.'

His face cleared. 'So that was why you stood me up. Of course. I should have realized there was an explanation. I should have listened to my daughter, who said at the time it was most unlike you. I'm afraid at times I can be obtuse.'

Megan was standing between them, silent, her eyes going from one face to the other.

'Dad, you mean to say you never got it sorted?'

'If you mean did I not phone Miss Loveridge, no. I thought I'd just been stood up. I decided . . . ' he grimaced.

'Trouble is, it doesn't happen to you often enough.'

'Megan!' he thundered.

Hetty, looking as appalled as she felt, was wondering how soon she could get away.

Megan dragged her toe across the pavement. 'So I suppose I really can't borrow the car this afternoon? I promise I'll be home by ten o'clock.'

Ignoring Megan's problem with the car because her own need to resolve her social gaffe was more pressing, Hetty said diffidently, 'The fault was mine, Mr Gillard. I should have remembered and let you know. At the very least I should have got in touch with you the following day.'

'Under such circumstances, how could an unimportant date be in the forefront of your mind? There's not even a need to apologize.' He turned his attention back to his daughter. 'Megan, you may not borrow the car. I told you, you must speak to Jit's parents first.'

'How is Jit?' asked Hetty. 'Such a nice girl with a real appreciation of poetry. I shall miss her next year.'

25

'Jit was one of your students, was she?'

'Not really. That is to say, Jit was doing maths because she has a place at Cardiff before doing a PGCE to teach. And I'm sure she'll get the grades they want. But she came to the book club with Megan. Have you seen her recently?' Hetty turned to Megan to ask anxiously, aware of a sudden and startling sense of foreboding.

'That's the whole point,' said Megan. 'I've not spoken to her at all since term ended.'

'Perhaps the family is on holiday.'

A large raindrop plopped on to the pavement between them, followed by another and another. 'It's going to rain,' said Tom, stating the obvious.

'That cloud is very menacing,' added Hetty, wishing she had brought her umbrella after all.

'Into the car,' urged Tom, sprinting for a low-slung, sporty-looking car parked conveniently nearby (one of the advantages of living in Otterhaven), his car keys in his hand. 'Quickly, both of you.'

Quite taken aback by the preemptory order, Hetty found herself in the front seat before she had time to object. 'Where are we going?' she asked a few moments later as Tom Gillard revved the engine and set off down the village street, his wheels splashing into the same puddle that had begun this sequence of events.

'Oops. Lucky no one was there this time.' He grinned at her, defying her to chide him. 'I'm taking you home.'

'Actually, I live in the opposite direction,' she said mildly, as Tom reached the edge of the village.

'Our home.' He flashed her a smile. 'That is, as long as you don't mind being kidnapped for lunch. We'll have an omelette and continue this interesting conversation regarding Jit. I like her, too. But I also remember a very formidable father.'

'You weren't doing anything more important, were you, Miss Loveridge?' asked Megan solicitously. 'I mean, Dad can be a little domineering sometimes.'

'Good word, that,' chuckled Tom. 'Domineering.'

'No, I've nothing better to do. Nothing that can't wait,' said Hetty hastily, aware how revealing that might have been. 'Nice car,' she said, stroking the squishy leather seat that betrayed evidence of venerable age.

'Dad has a thing about cars,' said Megan. 'That's why I don't have one myself.'

'Get yourself a degree, then we'll see,' said her father.

'That sounds fair,' agreed Hetty and saw

27

the flash of another smile on the man's face. 'Besides, cars can be a liability in a city.'

'Don't you drive, or don't you have a car?'

'Mother maintained that my car was an unnecessary expense. But, yes, I have an old and very reliable Nissan which I keep in a lock-up garage and drive mainly at weekends. I'd like to be able to say I use buses, but it's impractical in the country. I do ride my bicycle to school, though.'

'Your basket was always so heavy with homework we ran a book to see how long it'd be before you came off it.'

'Megan! Did you?'

'No, I didn't fall off,' said Hetty loftily.

'We ran the book for the two years of sixth form. Made quite a bit of money for charity.'

'I think I'll not ask which one.'

'Much better not, Miss Loveridge.' Yet again the smile was there.

'Do you think you might call me Hetty? Both of you.' She was amazed at the ease the request had emerged, for innate reserve — a shyness she had never been able to conquer except when she was with her students — preferred the formalities. Hetty settled into her seat for the drive to Gaer Hill. How good it was to have something to do that was utterly unforeseen.

                    ★   ★   ★

The omelette was fluffy, quite delicious; the poppy-seed rolls were freshly baked by the baker in Otterhaven. They had reached the coffee stage before Megan reverted to her plea to borrow the car to go and see her friend.

'Must I repeat myself? Only if you are invited by Jit's parents.'

'I love Mrs Singh. She's always so welcoming and Mr Singh is just the same. Jit is very lucky.'

Tom Gillard glowered at the implied criticism and Hetty, with some amusement, saw Megan glowering back.

'Mrs Singh's a fantastic cook, too. She said she'd teach me one day.' Megan was remembering the first time she'd visited the Singhs in Chepstow. She couldn't get over how British the house was, all chintz and ornaments. Weird. Though even then there had been that gorgeous smell of Indian cooking. Jit's mother was a large — well, motherly — woman who spent her whole time looking after her husband and agitating over the state of her daughter's welfare. Was she warm/cool enough? Had she eaten sufficiently? Had she done her homework?

Perhaps such maternal fuss could be too

much of a good thing, thought Megan, who had never known it and whose father would have found it incomprehensible.

'Mr Singh has a great sense of humour when he's in a good mood.'

'Any sense of humour might suffer failure if you turned up at an inconvenient moment,' her father pointed out.

'It would only be embarrassing if I arrived in the middle of the wedding.'

'What wedding would that be?' asked Hetty. 'I thought Jit was an only child.'

'Her brother is already married with two children. But I'm talking about Jit's wedding,' said the girl gloomily. 'I guess they've probably married her off by now as I haven't heard from her.'

'Good gracious!' exclaimed Hetty.

'Jit married? Do you mean that?' said Tom. 'I never knew she was engaged. She's only a schoolgirl. You must be wrong, Megan.'

'Jit told me there was a possibility her parents would insist on an arranged marriage for her as soon as she left school,' answered Megan. 'I just didn't believe it.'

★   ★   ★

Megan was aware that arranged marriages existed even in the twenty-first century.

30

Hadn't she seen *Monsoon Wedding* when it came out on DVD and thoroughly enjoyed it, without, it had to be admitted, realizing its implications?

'You are joking,' she said to Jit, her best friend at school, when Jit, with some diffidence, broke the news. 'Your father is insisting on an arranged marriage for you? He can't do that.'

It was during the exams and because they had time to kill before the next paper the two girls had gone into the village to distance themselves from the frantic atmosphere of near hysteria that prevailed among the rest of their class. They were sitting on the bench seat by the ancient weeping willow that trailed its fronds over the village duck pond, the ducks gathered at the far side where they were being fed by several little children.

'No joke,' said Jit.

'How long have you known about this?'

'Several weeks.'

With a pang, Megan absorbed the fact that she did not know everything about her friend.

'My father wants a double wedding with Balbiro at the end of the summer.' Balbiro was a first cousin of Jit's own age who lived and went to school in Bristol.

'But you are going to university in the autumn. The three of us are going to Cardiff.

31

I've already applied for student accommodation. I thought you had, too. Cool! Does that mean you'll be going as a married woman? Ah, I suppose that'll mean we won't be able to share after all.' Realizing that this comment must sound both selfish and naïve, Megan had the grace to blush. To cover her lapse she said, 'Married. Wow.'

'I'm not going to Cardiff,' said Jit gently. 'Nor is Balbiro.'

'That's nonsense. You and I both know we'll get our grades and from what you've told me about Balbiro, so should she.'

'It has nothing to do with grades. I suppose I've always known college was a dream that would never come true. I just didn't face up to it soon enough. School ends. Reality takes over from childhood. Mine does, anyway. A loving Sikh father has other ideas for his daughter's future.'

'What does your mother say?' asked Megan faintly, trying to adjust to the dismantling of their plans. Manjit Kaur had been brought to Britain as a young girl and had qualified as a doctor, though Megan did not think she had ever worked outside the home once she was married.

'My mother says that marriage is to be my career as it has been hers. She says that society is just too permissive for a young Sikh girl to live away from home. She insists that no Indian will take a wife with a dubious reputation and that no girl unprotected by her family could hope to have a good one. That's men for you, innit? Always expecting the worst. Ma says this marriage has to take place soon.'

'And you agree with her?'

'What choice do I have? S'pose she does have a point.'

Privately Megan considered that Jit had the option of refusal, but sensibly she thought that now was not quite the moment to mention it. 'What does Balbiro say?' Balbiro, who was even more striking to look at than Jit, was of a different temperament altogether. Megan had known her almost as long as she had known Jit and had visited her in her Bristol home on several occasions. But whereas Jit was docile and submissive, Megan had the distinct impression of a volatile nature, something of a rebel, in Balbiro.

'Balbiro says she will only marry a man of her choice,' replied Jit. 'Some chance. I think she will marry whoever they say.'

'You're not going to Punjab for these marriages, are you?' asked Megan suspiciously. She suddenly recalled reading about girls going to India for a supposed family visit only to be coerced into an arranged marriage there. Lurid visions of her friends being trapped into loveless relationships flashed through her mind.

'Goodness me, no,' said Jit, smiling. 'My father thinks it best for the marriages to happen here. And it's not as if it is happening tomorrow.'

★  ★  ★

Over coffee with her father and Miss Loveridge, Megan recounted this conversation haltingly, trying to remember nuances and Jit's facial expression.

'I mean, it was all so surreal. It was as if we were talking about another person altogether. Like a film script. But I don't think I really and truly believed it would ever happen. I mean, like, Jit's actually a month younger than me. Can you imagine me getting married?'

'You wouldn't dare,' said her father darkly.

'But that's just it,' said Megan. 'I'm eighteen. You couldn't actually do anything about it.'

'You may be sure I'd do my darndest.'

'But with Jit it's a matter of her being told she has to marry,' persisted the girl. 'It's not the same.'

'I must say I find it quite extraordinary.'

34

'Hetty, so do I.'

'Can't you do anything, Miss Lov — Hetty? I mean, you have influence.'

Hetty. Megan wondered if she would ever be able to bring herself to use the name, though she supposed it did suit her, in a funny sort of way. Miss Loveridge sounded so much like her, though. Prim. Remote. Formidable, if you were unfortunate enough to cross her. No, on second thoughts not remote, once you were in the sixth form. At the book club, for instance, Miss Loveridge had been surprisingly frank about emotions and how they coloured your life. Or how they had a negative effect on you if you did not control them. As if Miss Loveridge knew all about repression. Why had she obtained that impression? It was probably false, for look how relaxed Hetty was, sitting in the chair by the window with its stunning view across the valley towards the Black Mountains, where once again rain clouds were beginning to mass.

'Influence? I very much doubt it. But you said this happened in May?' prompted Hetty.

'During the exams. I've not seen anything of Jit since Speech Day. I spoke to her a couple of times. She didn't say very much, though. I did most of the talking. Dad wants to go to Scotland to do some painting and I don't, so I was sounding off to her.'

'Megan was resisting doing anything so uncool as agreeing to accompany her father on holiday,' said Tom.

'If Jit had offered information about her coming marriage I would have been happy to talk about that for hours,' Megan acknowledged ruefully. 'Do you think Jit is in any trouble?'

Hetty and Tom exchanged glances. 'Probably not,' said Tom, 'and even if she were, what do you think you could do about it?'

'Megan could hardly be expected to do anything,' said Hetty. 'On the other hand . . .'

'Yes?' Megan leaned forward.

'It would really mean that Megan had to borrow your lovely car.'

Tom Gillard raised his eyebrows. 'I do hope you are not suggesting that I should lend it to you to drive as an alternative?'

'No, indeed,' said Hetty, who disliked driving strange cars. 'But since I do not have my own car with me I shall have to be driven to fetch it.'

There was nothing in her tone of voice to suggest that she was put out by Tom's refusal to countenance her driving his car. Megan thought that her father had that predatory look about him that suggested he was becoming mildly interested in a woman. As in

Hetty, her teacher, a woman? Megan had been aware from the age of sixteen that her father had affairs. She knew that he thought she knew nothing about them. Quite untrue, though they were discretion itself and always conducted away from Otterhaven. And with younger women. Blondes, mainly. Still, she had come to recognize the signs: the frequent haircuts, the new clothes, the weekends when she was encouraged to take up an invitation to stay with friends. Like with Jit.

'So,' said Tom, crossing his legs, 'what exactly do you have in mind?'

'I remember promising to lend Jit a volume of Keats. We just happen to be in Chepstow . . . Perhaps we've been shopping?'

'In Chepstow?' Megan's voice expressed her extreme doubt that there could be anything worth her while purchasing in that particular town.

'Cribbs Causeway, then, and on the way back we — call in to see Jit.'

'Would you really?'

'A teacher never forgets a promise to one of her students,' Hetty said firmly. Inwardly, she was suddenly appalled by her rashness.

'I wonder how many agree with that old-fashioned attitude,' Tom Gillard threw in idly.

'A lot more would if school discipline

hadn't been shot to pieces by woolly-minded liberals of the politically correct variety,' snapped Hetty.

Tom Gillard sat up straighter. More than mildly interested, thought Megan, fascinated. 'May I, Dad?'

'May you what?'

'Borrow the car.'

'Oh, I suppose so,' he grunted. 'How long is this going to take?'

'If we left now,' said Hetty, 'we'd be in Chepstow in half an hour. Could we have finished our day's shopping in Cribbs Causeway by 3.30, do you think, Megan?' She named the newish shopping mall on the outskirts of Bristol.

Megan grinned. 'I expect I had a hissy fit, said there was nothing in the least fashionable there and refused to buy anything.'

'Not with me escorting you,' said Hetty. Her eyes were gleaming and her whole attitude was animated.

'This book you are going to lend Jit?'

'I happen to have a copy in my bag. I popped into Gerard's on my way to the butcher.' Gerard's was the secondhand bookshop in the village. Philip Gerard, who lived alone above the shop, was in his late fifties and was one of the few people who understood Hetty Loveridge. 'My copy of

Keats is a paperback that's falling to pieces and I decided to treat myself.'

'And did you really promise Jit you would lend it to her?'

'As it happens . . . Maybe it's a memory that is erroneous,' admitted Hetty. 'Does it matter?'

'I want to hear the outcome of this,' said Tom, as he picked up the car keys from the hall table, handing them to his daughter. 'Don't waste time by fetching Hetty's car, Megan. Use mine and take her home afterwards. Then come straight back and tell me all about your escapade. Though I expect there's neither a drama nor a crisis in Chepstow after all.'

★ ★ ★

Jit's family lived in a cul-de-sac of modern bungalows in the High Cross area of Chepstow. Megan Gillard and Hetty Loveridge sat in Tom Gillard's car without moving for a long moment after the girl had stopped the engine.

'Are you ready?' asked Hetty. 'I have the Keats here.'

'I suppose . . . '

'What do you suppose?'

'That Dad wasn't right after all?'

'That we shall be unwelcome? That at the very least we should have telephoned first?'

To Megan's relief there was only mild amusement in Hetty Loveridge's voice. 'I know, I deliberately don't take his advice sometimes. Quite often, in fact.'

'It would be the more surprising if you did take your father's advice,' the older woman said tartly. 'In my experience. Come on. We either get out of this car now — which, incidentally, you drive very well — or you drive off. Which is it to be?'

The front door was opened almost immediately by a grey-haired woman wearing the traditional *shalwar kameeza*, in shades of mauve and grey over which was a pale grey cardigan. 'Why, Megan, such a long time since we have seen you. Do come in.'

'Mrs Singh, I hope it's not inconvenient but we've been shopping and Miss Loveridge said she wanted to see Jit and as I wasn't able to telephone you first I thought we should just come.' It emerged in a rush.

Manjit Kaur, known at the school by her husband's name, and Hetty Loveridge merely smiled and waited. Megan had explained that with the Sikhs the women take the name Kaur because it means beautiful whereas the men are called Singh to mean brave, or a warrior, but that Sikh women often followed the British custom of using the man's surname by adding Singh to their names because it made life easier.

'Mrs Singh, this is Hetty Loveridge who teaches at the school. Miss Loveridge, this is Mrs Singh, Jit's mother. Sorry, I should have said that first.'

'Yes you should. Never mind. How do you do, Mrs Singh. In case this is very inconvenient, may I ask you just to give this book to Jit.' Hetty held out the Keats. 'I promised I'd lend her a copy. In fact, she may keep it, for I do have another at home.'

'You must give it to her yourself, Miss Loveridge. How good it is to meet you properly at last. I have heard so much about you and the book club from Jit. Now, Jit shall make us all a cup of tea while we get to know each other. Megan, please be so good as to fetch my daughter. She is in her bedroom. You know where it is. Miss Loveridge, please come this way.' Leading the way and talking all the time, Jit's mother went into the sitting-room.

★ ★ ★

Alone, the girls hugged silently. 'I can't believe you're here!' exclaimed Jit.

'I did try to phone you. You were switched

41

off the whole time. I texted every day to begin with. You didn't even text back.'

'I know. It is so good to see you.'

'You weren't . . . I mean, you aren't being coerced, are you?'

'That's a big word to use.'

'Are you being coerced, Jit?'

'Of course I'm not.'

'I must say you don't look as though you are particularly unhappy,' observed Megan, who thought her friend was looking really beautiful, her blue-black hair gleaming with health and vitality, her skin clear and her eyes sparkling.

'Of course I am not unhappy. Meg, what do you take me for? Come on, if they want tea, I'd better put the kettle on.'

As she followed her friend downstairs, Megan was struck by the contrast between them — though it was less apparent than when they were in school uniform for then Jit wore her school dress adapted to wear as a tunic over her *shalwar*, loose trousers caught in a band above the ankle. Today both girls were in jeans but whereas her own top was one of the popular skimpy camisoles embroidered with sequins and beads, Jit was more soberly clad in a plain white T-shirt.

'Then why didn't you at least text me?'

'Because there was nothing to say.'

'So you are coming to Cardiff with me in the autumn. That's great.'

'I am not going to uni.'

'Now we can arrange to live . . . What did you say?'

Jit placed a silver sugar bowl on the tray she was preparing. 'Will Miss Loveridge have Earl Grey or chai, do you suppose? Here, put these biscuits on the plate, will you?'

'Why aren't you going to uni?'

'Cos I'm getting married in July. I told you.'

'I didn't believe you, really. Who are you marrying?'

'His name is Sobha Singh. He comes from my father's village in Punjab and he is a distant relation. There was a photo of him. Actually they gave me three photos.'

'Of this Sobha Singh?'

'No, stupid. There were photos of three different men. One was very dark so I think my mother was glad I didn't choose him. One was — Oh, I don't know, I thought he looked shifty. Sobha looked — looks . . . quite nice. I've already met him, you see. I didn't change my mind.'

★   ★   ★

43

Over tea it emerged that the antecedents of Sobha Singh — his person, his character and habits — had been gone into minutely, long before the photograph had been handed over to Jit. Her family insisted that the young man was very suitable but only once Jit had approved — in principle only, Manjit Kaur insisted — were the arrangements set in train.

Balbir Singh, Jit's father and an accountant, as was Sobha himself, had found the young man a job in a factory producing garden furniture. He spoke little or no English and it would take some months of private tuition before he could take his first, junior place in the family accountancy firm in Cardiff. On the strength of this job and the impending marriage, the visa had come through without much delay.

'He is a good boy and he seems very smitten with Jit,' said Manjit Kaur. 'Though that was only to be expected.'

'Of course,' Hetty Loveridge agreed brightly.

'There is no pressure on Jit to marry. I hope you understand this,' said Manjit Kaur firmly. 'If my daughter had not liked the man her father had chosen for her, she would not be marrying him. On paper they seem well matched. Jit has agreed that an arranged marriage is what she wants. Her father would

44

have understood if she had refused Sobha after they had met.'

'That's all right, then,' said Hetty Loveridge. 'And exciting.'

Privately wondering if the beetle-browed Balbir Singh, whatever his sense of humour and his obvious affection for his daughter, would have proved to be as understanding as his wife made out, Megan said, 'Would it be all right to ask to see the photo?'

'I wonder, would both of you come to the wedding?' asked Manjit Kaur unexpectedly. 'It would give us all so much pleasure to see you there.'

# 3

'Do you suppose there's a reason why we've been invited to the wedding?' asked Megan, as they drove out of the cul-de-sac and away from the Singhs'.

'No, why should there be?'

'I don't know. It's just . . . I wondered . . . '

'Look, we'd better talk about this. There's a lay-by at the racecourse. Stop the car for a moment. You shouldn't be driving with your mind so preoccupied.'

Making a face, but doing as she was told, Megan pulled into the lay-by, stopped and switched off the engine. 'It's just that I've read a lot recently about forced marriages. I would hate to think that Jit was being made to marry by her family.'

'Do you have any reason for thinking that might be so?' asked Hetty cautiously. She did not regret her suggestion that she and Megan should visit Jit and the invitation to Jit's wedding had certainly come as an interesting surprise. Yet the last thing she wanted was to be involved in any criticism of the family's affairs.

'Jit laughed when I said that to her this afternoon.'

'There you are, then. Personally I was impressed by the way her mother insisted Jit could have refused the young man if she didn't like him. It all sounded perfectly genuine to me.'

'You saw Sobha Singh's photo. He's very dishy.'

'Do you think so? I suppose you're right.' Hetty sounded amused. 'All the more reason for accepting the wedding invitation. If it comes.'

'It'll come. What do you think I should wear?'

The discussion about clothes — might they be sitting on the floor? — occupied them both until they reached Otterhaven.

'Lucky you,' was her father's comment, when Megan handed back the car keys. 'Where's Hetty?'

'I took her home.'

'Oh. I thought dinner.'

'You should have said. It seemed the sensible thing to do, to take her home. Anyway, Miss Loveridge insisted.'

'I expect she was busy.'

He was interested, Megan thought. She hadn't expected that.

'I must say I envy you the experience of a Sikh wedding. You must make sure you take plenty of photos. I might even try a painting, if they're good. It would certainly be a different subject for me.'

Balbiro's journal, 20th April.
My name is Balbiro Kaur — though I am known as Balbiro Singh at school, because of the ignorance of the teachers who insist that I take the surname of my father. I am 18. Today my mother, Jasleen Kaur, told me that the date of my marriage has been set.

She also told me who I am to marry.

I come from a Sikh family that originated in Punjab. I was born in London and when I was small my family moved to Bristol where I also go to school. We see my aunty and uncle who live in Chepstow frequently and I am very fond of my cousin, Jit. Facts.

I have decided to keep an occasional journal about the matter of my marriage. Why? I am not sure that it will do any good, but I do it to relieve my feelings. Maybe when it is all over and there has been time to reflect I shall see where I was coming from and just maybe I will find the courage to go on.

You see? Already I am acknowledging that there is nothing I can do to prevent this happening.

For as long as I can remember I have wanted to be a doctor, like my Aunty Manjit, Jit's mother. Though unlike my aunty, I intended to continue with medicine once I was married. She was forced to give up her work when she got married. Forced? Do I mean that? I don't know, but it was the custom with us for a woman to give up work when she married. Of course I always knew I would marry, sometime. After I was qualified. All Sikh girls marry, eventually, and some much sooner than I think is right in the twenty-first century.

I made no secret of my aspirations, and whenever I talked at home about the courses I would do in the sixth form, and the grades I needed for university, my parents just smiled and nodded their heads in agreement. Jit and I planned to go to Cardiff where she would do a maths degree then become a teacher. Our fathers even signed the forms required by the school for our applications.

The last thing I expected was for my mother to tell me that there was to be no university, no qualifications in medicine.

'What need do you have of qualifications when you are married?'

'I don't want to be married,' I said stubbornly.

'Don't be a silly. All girls want to get married.'

'Well, I don't. I don't want to get married for years.'

My mother was scandalized. After, I wondered if it was genuine or was she, maybe, just a little bit envious that I could have ambitions?

Whatever, in the same stubborn way that I addressed her, my mother said, 'Your cousin, Jit, is to be married at the same time. It has all been decided by your families. There is to be a double wedding. It will be so fine.'

I could see that she was becoming very excited at the thought of all the shopping that would be involved. As if shopping could make up for the loss of a university education.

'I won't marry. I want to be a doctor.'

'Where will being a doctor get you? Nowhere. Don't you even want to know who you are marrying?' my mother asked slyly. 'Your father has approached the father of Resham Singh. It has been agreed. There, I knew you would be pleased.'

'I won't marry him.'

I was slapped for my pains. It was not a vicious blow though it did sting and afterwards there was a red mark.

I burst into tears but it was no use. Apparently there was to be no discussion. None whatever. When I met Jit a few days later, I was amazed to learn that she had three suitors to choose from. For me, it had been decided already. But for neither of us was there to be a university course.

I was to marry Resham.

Hetty Loveridge was in Scotland at last for her delayed holiday. She had planned to go away for a fortnight immediately term ended — as she usually liked to do since she always felt she needed a complete rest at the end of the school year — but there had been so much to do after her mother's death that she had been forced to put the holiday off. She had driven all the way, her Nissan having been thoroughly serviced beforehand, and had stopped for one night in Moffat before driving to Killearn, a small village not far from Loch Lomond, where she stayed for the weekend at the home of a former colleague with whom she had remained in contact.

Now she had just landed on the island of Mull. Hetty was a lover of islands, the smaller the better. Over the years she had got to know a few of the Scottish islands because her godmother lived on Mull and every couple of years Hetty visited Dorothy for a few days before going off on her own.

Dorothy Armstrong had known Joan Loveridge (Wentwood, as she was then) since they had met in Cheltenham where they were both training to teach. A firm friendship had developed between the two girls, which had survived all the years when their only contact had been letters. Dorothy had never married but she had been the obvious choice for godmother to Joan's only child. Hetty often wondered if it was perhaps because of the lack of her own children that Dorothy had been such a splendid godmother; generous to a fault with her birthday presents when Hetty was a child, a mediator between Hetty and Joan when in her early adulthood Hetty had schemes of which her mother disapproved.

Hetty remembered several holidays she and her mother had together spent with Dorothy on Mull. Dorothy had been born in Cumbria and once she had qualified she went back to teach in Whitehaven. Hetty did not know all the details but she gathered from oblique comments from Joan that there had been a young man to whom Dorothy had become engaged but who had found he preferred someone else only a week before their wedding. After the ensuing scandal Dorothy had decided to get away as far as possible from her roots and eventually she found a job as deputy head in Lancaster, where she remained until her retirement. It was then that she bought her small bungalow on the outskirts of Tobermory on Mull and where she had stayed ever since. In the years of her early retirement, Dorothy walked in the Lake District, the Pennines and on Skye. There were occasions when she went to Edinburgh for a few days to shop and visit the theatre. Other than that, Dorothy never travelled. She had a supportive circle of friends, many of whom came to Mull to visit her, not the least of whom were Joan and Hetty. Latterly, though, Joan had declined Dorothy's invitations saying that the journey was too tiring for old bones and, aside to Hetty, that anyway Dorothy's guest beds were far too soft and gave her a bad back.

'How good it is to see you!' Dorothy exclaimed as she embraced her goddaughter. 'You are looking peaky. And you've lost weight. Not surprising, I suppose. In fact, I was expecting something like this so I'm determined to fatten you up.'

'Fatten me, Godmother! I don't want to have to go and buy a whole new wardrobe — at least not until I start to think about winter clothes.'

'No?' Dorothy looked Hetty up and down and Hetty had the distinct impression that her godmother was not too favourably impressed. This was reinforced by her next comment. 'Well, I always thought you had a style that was years older than your age. Your mother's influence, I suppose. Still,' and Dorothy changed the subject, 'you've had a stressful time and you must have a good rest here. I'm so glad you are staying for a week. We have a lot of catching up to do. Now, let's not have any nonsense about polite reticence. I want to hear all about how you're coping since Joan died.'

Hetty smiled at her. 'It is good to be here

again. I feel relaxed already.'

Indeed she did. It had been hard in Otterhaven following her mother's death. Everyone knew Joan. Those who knew her best and liked her and who were frank about their own losses were the easiest to meet afterwards. Mere acquaintances and the inept (among whom she had thought to set Tom Gillard) could be unintentionally hurtful.

'So come and have a glass of whisky and tell me all about it. Did Joan really arrange her own funeral? She always said she would.'

'Down to the last hymn. Of course, she had chosen everything some time ago, but I don't think she had changed her mind in any way.'

'Joan was never one for changing her mind. She could be a bit obstinate. I hope you're not taking after her. Now,' said Dorothy, before Hetty had time to answer, 'how are you going to fill your time? Do you have plans?'

'The usual sort of thing. A little bit of walking, possibly a trip to Iona if the weather holds and you don't mind if I desert you for one night. Or will you be coming with me this time?'

'Most unlikely and certainly not to Iona. I don't care for it nowadays. Far too touristy for my tastes. I shall stay at home, do my garden and prepare something delectable for

54

your tea when you return.'

'You must let me take you out for a meal.'

'Whatever for? I buy good, fresh ingredients. No point in paying the earth for some man in a poncey white hat to cook them.'

Hetty smiled again, thinking that Dorothy never changed. 'You know, sitting here listening to you, it might be my mother speaking. No wonder you got on so well.'

'There were times when we had our differences. Did I ever tell you . . . '

Out came an old photograph album and Dorothy began reminiscing. Lulled by the whisky and the care, Hetty felt her anxieties fade into insignificance. As long as you had sympathetic human contact somewhere in your life, it was still worth living.

★  ★  ★

From Tobermory it was possible to take a boat trip to Iona for the day — a long day and one that gave you just enough time to stretch your legs and see the abbey. Hetty preferred the long car journey through the length of Mull to Fiannphort, where the little ferry took foot passengers across. There you could stay the night and drink in the atmosphere, for once the daytrippers had gone home it was incredibly peaceful and the night sky — when it was clear — was full of the brightest stars you could imagine.

The weather stayed fine and after a very early start Hetty had parked her car and was on Iona well before lunchtime. She checked in to the Argyll, one of the two small hotels, then she took a picnic lunch off to her favourite spot where she could sit undisturbed, read a book or simply look at the birds. This time she was dismayed to find that her most preferred rock for leaning against was already occupied — at least the area in front of it was — by an artist, a man who had set up his easel for the view across to Mull and who was so absorbed by his work that he was unaware of Hetty's arrival.

She admired that: total preoccupation in an endeavour that rendered a man oblivious to all that was going on around him, even though on this occasion she was inconvenienced. Hetty shook her head, but he had got there first and a bit further on there was another nook that took in much the same view and was equally idyllic. She turned away to reach this spot by a circuitous path, unwilling to disturb the artist, though she would have liked to have seen his style; to have seen if he had captured any of the beauty of what was in front of them, or if he were merely a clumsy amateur.

Except for the artist, who was only a couple of hundred yards away from her, Hetty was alone. It was peaceful yet not silent, for there was the constant murmur of the sea and the raucous cries of the birds, common gulls and a pair of little Arctic terns, wheeling in the air or bobbing on the water. Several gulls came to stand on the beach in a wide circle in front of her, beady eyes alert for other scavengers while each anticipated the chance of a morsel of her lunch.

It was an hour or so later when she heard a footfall above her, a crunch of a foot on small stones one of which was dislodged and fell beside her with a plop.

'Hey, I'm so sorry. I do hope that didn't hit you,' a startled male voice said.

Hetty half-turned and stared up into a familiar face. It was Tom Gillard, clad in an old pair of shorts and an open-necked shirt with its sleeves rolled up and encumbered by a portfolio and various bags, which presumably carried his easel and paints.

'Hello,' he said, scrambling down the rock and propping his artist's paraphernalia carefully against the rock beside her. 'I never expected to find you here.'

'Are you the artist who was occupying my favourite rock?'

'Oh, Lord.' He smacked his forehead in

57

mock dismay. 'Not only have I tried to injure you, I've spoilt your day. Now you won't even speak to me.'

'I've already spoken to you,' she pointed out, amused.

'In a very accusatory voice.'

'I beg your pardon. Won't you sit down?'

'I thought you'd never ask.' He flopped down beside her. 'The stone didn't hit you?'

'No. I'm quite unscathed. What are you doing here?'

'Painting. As you saw.'

'Do you come here often?' She groaned inwardly at the ineptitude of her social skills when faced by a man who must surely still remember how she had stood him up — even though it was inadvertent.

'No,' he answered gravely. 'This is the first time I have come to Iona, though I've been to Scotland once before, to the Outer Hebrides — don't we call them the Western Isles now? I enjoyed that, especially South Uist. The light is very different from home, which is one of my reasons for coming here — to explore how light changes even though the scenery is much the same. You know, sea, sand, rocks, dunes. Light and cloud make all the difference.'

'So you don't just paint local Welsh scenery?'

'Not at all. You'd become a boring artist if you never tried anything diverse. Most of my seascapes come from Pembrokeshire but I've painted in the south of France and in Majorca. You have to be a bit careful not to paint too much exotica because of your sales, you see. Local views sell better in their locality, which may sound as if I'm a bit of a Philistine but though I'm an artist, I still have to make a living.'

'How very pragmatic.'

'I thought you'd disapprove.'

'Not at all. I beg your pardon, I really didn't mean to criticize. I mean, I know so very little about any of this.'

'But you are not totally ignorant of my world. You know enough to buy a painting.'

'I know what I like.' She smiled at him broadly. 'You might as well know it — I'm not an admirer of modern art. I think the last exhibition I totally enjoyed was the Pre-Raphaelites. Now sneer.'

'Oh dear. I think maybe I should do something about your artistic education, or am I coming over as an ogre?'

It struck Hetty that the suggestion that Tom might even consider educating her meant that he contemplated spending time with her. It gave her a frisson of pleasure even

59

while she was dismissing the notion as absurd.

'Do you have to catch a ferry this afternoon,' she asked, 'or are you staying the night? I mean, are you on your way back to the ferry?'

'I'm staying at the Argyll. There didn't seem any point in coming to Iona for only an hour or so. Between you and me, I think I preferred painting on Caldey Island. There's the Welsh for you. Insular.'

'Are you Welsh?'

'Second generation. Not sure if that counts or not. So, I set up where you found me and now I feel like trying the same picture from a different angle. Are you just here for the day?'

'No. I'm staying at the same hotel.'

'Good. We'll have dinner together. But now I'm going to leave you to your book. I'm only half on holiday, you see. Got a picture to paint. See you, Hetty.'

With that he picked up his stuff and walked away.

Hetty blinked, unsure whether to be eager for their next meeting or a little annoyed that her tranquillity had been disturbed. Most definitely her tranquillity had been disturbed. She felt energized, no longer the rather melancholy woman who had set foot on the island not so long ago. How very strange that she should have met Tom Gillard yet again and so far from home ground. She wondered if he felt the same.

* * *

That evening they shared a platter of locally caught grilled fish and a bottle of Chardonnay and their conversation never once faltered, one subject slipping naturally into the next so that Hetty was amazed that two whole hours had passed before they were ready to leave the table.

After dinner Tom suggested that they should go for a walk. Hetty, whose shoes were sensibly flat, agreed immediately and they set off in the opposite direction from where they had met in the morning. Though it was not long after nine o'clock they were far enough north for it still to be sufficiently light to see where they were going. Only under the stunted trees were there shadows and the trees themselves were thrown into stark relief.

'I don't think we shall need a torch,' said Tom, 'but I have one just in case.'

'A practical man. So have I.'

It was very peaceful; lights were already shining through the windows of most of the cottages and occasionally there was the bark of a dog alerted to their passing but otherwise there was no noise save for the scrunch of their shoes on loose grit. The lane they were on was bordered by dry stone walls, which harboured wild flowers: purple foxgloves, harebells which were known as the Scottish bluebell, yellow hawkbit and the pink herb robert.

'Isn't it beautiful?' said Tom. 'I've always wanted to live on a remote island like this.'

'Then why haven't you?'

'Oh, you know: impractical, too far from anywhere, Megan to consider. I could never have sent her to boarding school and that is probably what would have happened if I had indulged myself. Besides, I wonder if I would have done so much work without the pressures of a gallery behind me. I think one could easily succumb to sloth on an island.'

'I suppose there is always that possibility. It mightn't be quite so idyllic in the winter, either. At least not in this part of the world.'

'Have you ever visited your godmother in the winter?'

Hetty had told Tom all about Dorothy, had even toyed with the notion of asking Tom to come to tea with them, but shyness prevented her — at least before she had spoken to her godmother. Tom was staying on Mull for another two days. 'No,' she replied. 'My mother and I sometimes went to Madeira

62

during the February half-term for some sunshine. Mother's back didn't like the damp.'

'So you were not in the habit of going off on your own?'

'No, indeed.' Hetty sounded quite shocked. 'That is to say, there were a few courses I went on, to do with school, naturally, but I could never leave my mother for very long. She had a hard life with my father dying so young and I felt . . . '

'That you had to make it up to her?'

'Please don't use whatever knowledge of psychology you have to come to the conclusion that my mother was manipulating me,' she said sharply.

'I wouldn't dream of suggesting that a woman such as you, obviously highly intelligent, wouldn't have seen through that.'

'I mean, Mother and I got on so well together. So — we relied on each other for companionship.'

'Yet Mrs Loveridge had her own interests.'

'Certainly. She played bridge regularly and did a lot for the church so she knew most people of her own age in Otterhaven.'

'She was a lucky woman.'

That Tom thought her mother was probably an old witch was as clear as if he had spoken the words. It was untrue and unfair of him. Though one comment had struck her forcefully.

'I've never thought of my mother in that way before — I mean as being lucky,' said Hetty. 'I suppose that in a way you are right. How strange.'

They had stopped walking and were standing by the low stone wall facing each other. Hetty's countenance was troubled — not only from what he had said but because she had become unaccountably heated. Flushes, she had thought, were a thing of the past.

'I'm pleased that I might have persuaded you to re-evaluate your relationship with your mother. These things are necessary once in a while.' He stopped, shrugged, then took a deep breath. 'For heaven's sake, woman, you have a good chunk of your life in front of you. Don't waste it grieving for that part of it which has been wrapped in cotton wool.' Without touching her with his hands, Tom bent towards her.

Afterwards Hetty did not have the least idea whether he was actually going to kiss her or whether she had read far too much into a movement. She jerked away from him as though from the sting of a wasp and at that moment an owl hooted, its call long and low. A dark shape flew across the narrow road at shoulder height, just feet from Tom's head.

Hetty gasped. 'What — what was that?'

'Only an owl. You must have heard an owl before?'

There was a note of exasperation in his voice which made her cringe.

'I'm not used to seeing one quite so close,' she said defensively.

A smattering of cloud was drifting across the sky, draining the light, and as it did so a small breeze got up. Hetty shivered as her heated flesh cooled too rapidly.

'I think I should like to go back now,' she said in a small voice.

'You're getting cold.'

'Just a little.'

'Would you like my jacket?'

'Of course not. That is, thank you, but you will need it yourself. When we start walking again I shall warm up quickly enough.'

'As you say.'

The mood of the evening had altered dramatically. There was absolutely no way of rectifying it, Hetty could sense that. What a fool she was. Would it have been so very terrible if Tom Gillard had actually kissed her? She could hardly remember the last man to have done so. That is, she could and it had not been in the least enjoyable. It had been in Llandrindod Wells, at the end of a long weekend course in some arcane subject. Like her, he (she couldn't even remember his name) taught English. Hetty had got the impression that he did not much like his job and was only marking time before he took early retirement, though he had been quite interesting on the subject of playwriting, at which he was a failure. (In her opinion, though not in his.) He had grabbed her by the lift when they reached their floor and in that instant she had known very well how the evening was supposed to end, and where.

That she had gone to bed alone and unscathed had said a lot about her ability to appear to misunderstand innuendo. On reflection she realized he might have been relieved that nothing had happened between them after all, for she did not think she would have been rated much of a conquest.

Hetty thought that in the morning Tom Gillard would feel a sense of relief in much the same way. At least she could encounter him in the middle of Otterhaven in the future without feeling any confusion.

They had reached their hotel without another word having been spoken.

'Good night, Hetty.' Tom collected both their keys and handed hers over. 'Thank you for an agreeable evening.'

'Yes, indeed,' she replied. *Agreeable!* she was thinking.

'I hope we may repeat it some other time.' There was a glint in his eye that was not lost on her.

'I think I shall be occupied with my godmother for the remainder of my stay,' she said primly.

'Of course you will be. I was referring to your return to Otterhaven. There is unfinished business between us, I believe.'

'Unfinished . . . ' She gulped.

'Your artistic education,' he said smoothly. 'I'm determined you will find one artist to admire who is post Pre-Raphaelite.'

'G-good night, Tom,' Hetty said, and almost ran down the corridor, defying Tom to so much as chuckle and resisting the urge to turn and see his knowing smile follow her to her room.

# 4

'Was Iona as idyllic as ever?' Dorothy asked. 'I think you've caught the sun.'

'I sat reading on the beach yesterday, then this morning I walked. Such luck to have the weather for it.'

'Did you eat at the hotel?'

'I had a very pleasant meal,' said Hetty, thinking that most of her evening had been delightfully unexpected. 'Would you believe it? I shared my table with someone I'd met in Otterhaven only recently. A parent of one of my girls.'

'One of your girls. How very Miss Jean Brodie. Would that have been by design or merely a coincidence?'

'Excuse me?'

'Did you just share the table or did he ask you to have dinner with him?'

'He asked . . . ' Hetty fell into the trap neatly.

'So I'm right in assuming this parent is the father.' Dorothy grinned in triumph. 'Well, that was nice.'

'Such an all-inclusive word,' Hetty said. 'Nice. Do you know it is one of the most difficult expressions to eradicate from a student's writing?'

'Then define 'nice' in this context for me.'

'As I said, pleasant. The meal was simple but well cooked. We shared a bottle of delicious wine. Stimulating. Tom is very easy to talk to.' Hetty considered the descriptive words she had used: pleasant, delicious, stimulating, easy . . . He was easy to talk to, until she began to feel threatened. Hetty began to think that she should not be quite so critical in future about the use of the word 'nice'.

'Nice, indeed,' said Dorothy mockingly. 'Have you known this Tom for a long time?'

'I met him this summer. He is an artist and I had just indulged myself by buying one of his paintings. You see, I hadn't met him when I bought his painting. I bought that merely because I liked it. Tom says that art is like literature. You should invest in it whenever it pleases you.'

'That could be an expensive pastime,' Dorothy said drily. 'What does this Tom paint?'

'Watercolours. Mainly local scenes, local as in around South Wales. I bought one he had painted of the Blorange. But Tom — that is, Tom Gillard, though you probably won't have heard of him — has come to Mull to experiment with light and shade in his work.' She was remembering with a pang that the painting she had bought with such elation was still in its wrapping by her chest of drawers. Hetty had not had the heart to hang something that she had acquired almost as an act of rebellion, acquiring it on the very day her mother died. Yet paintings were meant to be seen, to be hung on a wall and enjoyed. What was it Tom had accused her of? Spending her time grieving for that part of her life which had been wrapped in cotton wool.

'You have gone very quiet. Did this Tom upset you in any way?'

'He said something that made me cross at the time.' Hetty told Dorothy defensively that Tom obviously thought Joan had manipulated her for the best part of her life. 'The very idea that I always did exactly as my mother wanted. It's ludicrous.'

'It may be ludicrous to you but it seems to me this Tom has judged the situation excellently.'

'Godmother Dorothy! You can't mean that.'

'Well, only you really know the truth of the matter,' answered Dorothy reasonably, 'but you must admit you fell in with your mother's wishes most of the time. It did seem to me

70

that you had very little life of your own.'

'It isn't true,' said Hetty weakly. An old witch. Here was another person, Joan's oldest friend, coming to the same conclusion as someone who had never even met her. Yet perhaps there was some truth in it after all. Then, had it done her so much harm not to have been self-assertive? She and her mother had cared for each other. Was this so very unnatural? Had she really missed out on life? Hetty could not think this must be so.

'As I say, it is what you believe that matters. Now, I've prawns for tea. Do you want a bath first or a whisky?'

'Do you know, I feel like both at the same time.'

'Excellent,' said Dorothy, ignoring Hetty's aggressive tone. 'Just what I should have suggested. Pour yourself a good measure and take it up to the bathroom. We'll eat in half an hour.'

★   ★   ★

The dishes from their meal having been put away by Hetty, Dorothy broached the subject she had been wanting to mention ever since her goddaughter's first appearance in Tobermory. 'I hope Joan has left you reasonably well off?'

'Her pension stops, of course, but once probate is through the house is mine. I mean, literally mine. I'm lucky because the mortgage was cleared some years ago.'

'You won't think of selling, I imagine?'

'You wouldn't credit how many have already asked me that.'

'With a view to buying the property cheaply, I suppose. People can be very single-minded when it comes to their own interests.'

'I wouldn't dream of moving. The cottage is so convenient, both for school and the shops, and it is not so very large for me on my own.'

'That's sensible. Pulling up your roots can be extremely painful.'

'And as far as I am concerned there is no point in pulling up my roots. I know you speak from experience,' said Hetty, 'but when you got your deputy headship that was a career move, which is quite different from any move that I could think of making. Head of department is quite sufficient for my ambitions.'

'It might have been a career move for me: nevertheless, it was necessary.' Dorothy grimaced. 'Did Joan ever tell you what really happened?'

'Only that you had a failed engagement

and decided you needed to move away from your home town. It must have been very difficult for you.'

'It was the worst time of my life.' There was a pause for a moment. Then Dorothy said, 'A few days before the wedding I discovered that Alan, my fiancé, had made one of my bridesmaids pregnant.'

'Godmother . . . How absolutely dreadful!'

'It was shattering. Of course I couldn't marry him then, though he swore it was all a mistake and it was me he loved.'

'The rat.'

'My father was all for horse-whipping him. Joan, who was my chief bridesmaid, probably agreed with Father. She said I had to cut Alan out of my life immediately. They were all very protective of me: my father, the rest of my family, Joan. But I insisted that I should see Alan just the once after it all came out. You can imagine that all I really wanted was to get away from the stares and the comments.'

'It must have been sheer hell.'

'Only to be expected in those days. As it happens, I was fortunate. My headmaster — who had already heard about the catastrophe before I went to see him — was sympathetic and arranged for me to exchange with a teacher from another school for the following term. He admitted that this was entirely in his interests. In those days most women didn't continue their teaching career after they were married. I had given in my notice but my headmaster hadn't found my replacement. So immediately the summer term started and I was settled at the new school, I began looking for a permanent job. Again I was fortunate and very quickly I found the school and the position I wanted and there I stayed for the rest of my working life.'

'Did you never think of returning home?'

'Lancaster had become my home by then. My parents retired to Keswick after a few years because they loved the Lake District, though I think they never got over what they called my shame. At the same time my sister married and went to live in Kirby Lonsdale so all my family was within a reasonable distance. Besides . . . ' Dorothy hesitated. 'There is a reason why I am telling you all this. You see, though I refused to marry Alan, I realized all too soon that I did still love him and was broken-hearted from calling off our marriage. He never did marry my bridesmaid and I always wondered if what he had told me about loving me was the truth and if, one day, he would come to find me. It seemed best to stay in one place so that the possibility would always be there.'

'Good heavens,' said Hetty faintly. 'Did . . . I mean . . . did you ever make any attempt at contacting him?'

'Of course I didn't,' her godmother answered with asperity. 'Women didn't do that sort of thing in my day.' She sighed. 'I don't know. Maybe it was for the best. Eventually Alan married a woman much older than himself, but I heard that it didn't last. I don't know what became of him. But what I am trying to say to you is that now that Joan has gone you have to take hold of your life. You mustn't allow yourself to be controlled by events.'

'As I was controlled by my mother?'

'I expect it made for an easy, comfortable life.'

'I suppose it did,' Hetty said slowly, 'but is there anything so very wrong in that? Besides, as for change, I should have thought that losing my mother was quite bad enough. I need space.'

'You can't lock yourself away because you have been bereaved. You have to move on, accept challenges.'

'What challenges?' Hetty cried in exasperation. 'Godmother, you are not making sense. I have my own home. I have a very good job. I have some excellent friends. I have a healthy bank balance and an adequate pension to look forward to. What else should I need?'

'A man in your life?'

'Don't you dare say I need a husband.'

'Not if you don't want one. But what do you do when you come home in the evening and shut the door behind you? At the weekends, the school holidays? Now that your mother is dead will you go on just as before, except without her? Tell me, when did you last do anything really stimulating?'

Hetty was thinking that her visit to Iona had been one of the more invigorating events that she had experienced recently. Tom Gillard had made it so, though not for the world would she have admitted it. 'I don't have time, with my job,' she said, after a pause. 'Homework to mark, lessons to prepare. You of all people should know that.'

'And you play no bridge and walk on your own. Hetty, you must not become a recluse. You have to take up something interesting.'

'Like what?'

'Learn a foreign language. Take up salsa dancing.'

'Salsa . . . '

'Do some volunteering.'

'Charity work.' The words were loaded with scorn.

'What's wrong with helping other people?'

Too late Hetty remembered that Dorothy

helped in a charity shop in Craignure and when she was younger she had been a team leader for the WRVS emergency services. 'No time,' she replied defensively.

'There is always time, if you want to do something badly enough, or if you are sufficiently motivated.'

'I'm going to a Sikh wedding at the end of the month,' Hetty said defensively.

'How splendid. On your own?'

'No. I'm going with Tom Gillard's daughter.'

'You must write and tell me all about it.'

Balbiro's Journal, 27th April

I have known Resham Singh since my first day at primary school. I remember being terrified that day. It was all so big, so new, so different. The only consolation was that I was with my cousin, Jit. There were other Sikhs at the school, which was in London, boys as well as girls. The girls were all right. Some of them were quite friendly. The boys I was not so sure about. They all seemed so big and noisy. There was one boy in particular who was a year or so older than us. I tried very hard to keep away from him in the playground. Not that the boys and girls played together. But if he found himself near me, Resham pulled my plaits. Always.

I don't think Resham was really unkind. I began to notice that he never let any of the other boys so much as talk to me. I remember one afternoon when Resham found an English boy making fun of me, calling me names. Resham went red in the face with fury and there was a fight. Resham would have got into terrible trouble if I hadn't said that this other boy (I've forgotten his name) was bullying me. Then it was all right.

A few years after that we moved to Bristol. I missed some of my friends, of course, but it could have been much worse. As Aunty Manjit and Uncle Balbir had moved to Chepstow at about the same time I knew I would see Jit frequently.

In Bristol the new Gurdwara we attended on special days was quite near our new house (which was much bigger than our old one). To my surprise, one of the first people we saw at the Gurdwara was Resham and his family. By then I knew that our families were related, but no one had said they were moving, too. Our two fathers had become friends, my mother said when I asked.

I can't say that I actually met Resham after my twelfth birthday, except to see him across a room — I was always with the women and the only people I was ever allowed to talk to were the other girls. But Resham smiled back at me, when no one was watching. I suppose I got used to his smile and I felt something was missing when he wasn't there.

How could my parents have decided that this boy is to be my husband?

78

Hetty did not see Tom Gillard again. She did not know where he was staying, had not asked, and apart from two short walks in the rain — for the weather had changed — Hetty confined her sightseeing to shopping in Tobermory. Dorothy said her knees were playing her up and that she would prefer to keep out of the bad weather.

Hetty said her thank yous and goodbyes with real appreciation for the company and the affection which now was missing in her life. Both women promised to keep in touch regularly — which Hetty knew meant letter writing because Dorothy had never been one to talk endlessly on the telephone. Hetty certainly intended to keep her promise, even if her letters were not all that lengthy.

One of the first things Hetty did when she returned to Otterhaven was to hang Tom Gillard's picture of the Blorange, moving a print of Otterhaven's churchyard from above the mantelpiece in the sitting-room. It had been one of her mother's favourites but Hetty had always thought it a very gloomy subject and now that Joan's ashes were to be buried in that same churchyard beside her father she decided she wanted to have something more uplifting displayed where she would see it every day.

Hetty had taken a print of Cheltenham to

her godmother knowing it would bring back memories (and a few tears) and also a willow-patterned plate which she thought was too whimsical (and Dorothy had collected them for years). Her mother's clothes still had to be sorted but after the break Hetty felt more able to face that job, taking the better conditioned clothes to the Save The Children shop — and recalling Dorothy's strictures on volunteering as she entered the premises.

No. She did not want to serve behind a counter, she concluded as she left the premises.

There were not many other changes at home that Hetty contemplated. Joan had a small bed in the garden where she grew salad crops: a few lettuces, some tomatoes and a few runner beans because she said they tasted so much better than the shop-bought ones. This Hetty planned to put to easily maintained shrubs. She had a feeling her mother would be spinning in her grave once the last of her vegetables had gone, but with a good, old-fashioned greengrocer in the village it seemed a waste of Hetty's time to grow her own. She would, though, grow herbs just outside the kitchen door, Hetty decided, in a decorative tub (another of her mother's hates). Hetty herself was something of a novice about gardening and supposed that she would have to read her mother's books and learn the best time of the year to do the pruning, which she could see would make up the bulk of her work, there being no grass to mow in their small garden.

Wine glass in hand, Hetty stood on the terrace and considered what she was going to do next. It was true what Dorothy had said: there was going to be time on her hands despite her schoolwork and while she did not want to sell second-hand clothes for charity or turn out in the middle of the night to feed survivors of an emergency, the idea of voluntary work did have some appeal. The local paper that week had contained an article written by one of the trustees of a small, walled garden which was part of the estate of the Norman castle nearby and which, though it had passed through several families in the course of its history, continued to be in private ownership. This walled garden was now maintained by volunteers. 'Any help, skilled or otherwise, would be greatly appreciated,' had been the final plea.

It would be exercise (salsa dancing, huh!). She would work in the company of other people (yet she would not be required to converse while she was working). As a by product, from time to time she could even ask advice about her own garden. She would offer that very evening, before she had second thoughts.

'Try us a few times before you make a regular commitment,' the trustee in charge of the garden suggested. His name was Clive Makepeace. He'd meet her the following morning, which happened to be a Saturday.

'That would probably be my most convenient time. Not every week, I think,' Hetty said cautiously.

'We should be so lucky,' said Clive. 'See how it goes. We have a useful team this week. That'll be six of us. There are branches of a dead tree to clear away and once that has been done the ground to dig over. Do you have your own tools?' He suggested what she might bring. 'Most women prefer to bring something they're familiar with. Less likely to develop blisters.'

Blisters, Hetty thought, horrified that she hadn't thought the consequences through. Two men and three other women. She wondered if she knew any of them.

The castle was isolated, five miles outside Otterhaven, standing just below the brow of a hill which sheltered it from the east (the English side) and gave commanding views over to the Brecon Beacons from where, presumably, the enemy Welsh would have been expected to make their attack.

82

Hetty parked her car beside several others and joined the little group by the old wooden garden gate. They turned as one to greet her.

'Hello,' said a well-preserved man of indeterminate age, his hand out stretched. 'I'm Clive. We spoke yesterday.'

'Hello. I've brought what you suggested. What do I need first?'

'Hi, Hetty. Bring your gloves and some secateurs and I'll initiate you into the back-breaking job of clearing up debris. If we really get going we can make ourselves a bonfire. I love a bonfire.'

It was Tom Gillard.

'Sadly bonfires are not always politically correct nowadays,' said Clive. 'So you know each other?'

Hetty got the distinct impression that Clive was not too pleased about this. 'Yes. We've met,' she said cautiously. She had not seen Tom's car parked with others, though now she came to think about it, one had been half-hidden by a tree. Would she have stayed if she had realized he was there?

'Do you know Jane . . . Sheila . . . and Wendy . . . ?'

'How do you do?'

The women were all elderly. Hetty suspected they were all very keen gardeners, knowledgeable and fit. She could always disappear after one morning, she thought.

'Come and see our domain.'

The garden was just over two acres and behind stone walls, which were in a good condition. Hetty was told later that in the district there was a young man who had set himself up as an expert in repairing ancient dry stone walls and who occasionally gave his services free to the Trust. The garden, known as The Grange, was not large as gardens went but its layout was historic. In it there had been a knot garden containing herbs, a pond, a pleached walk, some topiaried box and an expanse of beds. Some of the structure was still apparent but in the main most of the area was uncultivated except for a few decrepit fruit trees and an expanse of lawn.

'Historically speaking the lawns are quite wrong,' Clive said ruefully. 'We should have vegetable beds, flower beds for cutting, fruit trees, cold frames, a heated greenhouse and a vinery, not to mention any number of proper potting sheds.'

'Whoa,' said Sheila. 'Hold your horses, Clive. If you had half a dozen able-bodied men you might be able to cope with all that. As it is, be thankful we have been able to restore just the one shed. You'll find, Hetty, that it comes in very handy in the winter for a cup of tea, even if this slave driver thinks we should be out in all weathers.'

'Please don't put Hetty off before she's even started,' Tom groaned. 'Come on, let's get going.' He led her to the far side of the garden where a gnarled apple tree lay on the ground.

'How sad,' said Hetty, regarding the tree. It was the first time she had addressed Tom directly.

'Yes. I suppose so. But there's a time for everything and this tree fell last winter. See how rotten the trunk was? Clive thinks we might be able to sell the wood for firewood and if we do it'll pay for some replacement stock.'

'Oh dear,' said Hetty. 'You all sound so well informed and I'm terribly ignorant about all of this.'

'Don't give it a thought. Everyone knows far more about all this than I do,' Tom said airily. 'I'm just a pair of hands. Sheila is an expert, but Wendy doesn't know a weed from a flower. Jane keeps very much to herself except when Clive needs another pair of hands.'

'I'm not sure that I am more than a pair of hands. Soft ones at that,' murmured Hetty.

'Nor am I. As far as I'm concerned, a weed is only a weed if it's in the wrong place. If it looks pleasing I leave it where it is.'

Hetty laughed. 'I guess that's what I shall have to do.'

'Just ask if you aren't sure what's what. As for this morning, look, cut the smaller stuff into manageable lengths and cart it in this bag over to the bonfire. I hope you're not allergic to smoke.'

'Actually I love a bonfire, too, but we aren't permitted to light one in the village. Politically incorrect, as Clive said.'

'Not where I live, thank goodness.' For a time they worked together in silence.

When they stopped for a short break — Hetty wondering just how unfit she actually was — she commented, 'I didn't imagine I'd find you here.'

'Or you might not have offered your services?' He grinned at her to take away the sting of his words.

'I'd have thought you might be wary of damaging your hands.'

'I do nothing without really good gloves. It's interesting work and you may have noticed that my garden is quite small. Besides, the exercise is good for me. Have you seen inside the castle?' he asked, changing the subject.

'No, never.'

'The Beresfords who own it now are an interesting couple. You must meet them sometime. I'm sure they'd be only too delighted to show you over their home.'

Infinitesimally there had crept between them the same easiness that had been apparent from their first meeting, when Hetty had lunched with Tom and Megan and when the two of them had dined together on Iona. Hetty relaxed into the physical work, pleased with herself and what she was doing and convinced that whatever tension had come between herself and Tom in Scotland had now been resolved.

'Will we see you next week?' asked Clive, as they returned to the cars. 'Oh, no. You said you could only make it once a fortnight.'

'I'm going to a wedding next Saturday. The week after would be fine,' said Hetty.

'That'll do us very nicely.' They all drifted towards the cars.

'Of course, it's your Sikh wedding with Megan,' said Tom. 'She's very excited about it.'

'So am I,' said Hetty.

'Have you decided who's driving?'

'I've offered to pick Megan up at 11.30. I've no idea what time we'll be back.'

'I'll plan a simple supper for all of us. If you've eaten too well at the wedding it won't matter in the least if you're not hungry.'

'That's very kind. I'll look forward to it.'

# 5

Balbiro's Journal, 4th May

Resham Singh arrived at our home promptly for the meeting that was to signify our agreement to be married. It is said that our girls are not forced to marry but once it had been decided that my marriage was to take place there was no question but that it was to be Resham. I thought that was unkind. I thought I should at least have been consulted.

I had been permitted to choose my outfit and decided on the pink which I thought was most flattering. Why did I want to look my best? Why do you think ... Whatever I might feel about Resham, I was determined that nothing should go wrong that day which they could say was my fault. Resham, wearing a smart suit, was more handsome than ever. I had not seen him for six months.

I wondered, did he want this? Was he as much against the match as I? Then surely he would be protesting. Why had no one told him I wanted to go to university before there was any talk of marriage? Had anyone even mentioned that I was unwilling?

Resham and I were not left alone for a minute.

88

Always his mother, or mine, was hovering near the open door. When they'd all gone I cried and said I'd never be forced into marriage. My father left the room. My brother, Keval, told me I was a fool. My mother slapped me. Again.

That surprised me, that Keval approved of the marriage. At school they had been best friends but recently I had heard Keval say disparaging things about Resham. I'd even thought my brother might be on my side. How wrong I was!

If Resham had given me just one small hint that he wanted this marriage, even then I think I might have abandoned my fight. Why is it that our parents show us the wide world then snatch it from us when we reach out to grasp it with our hands?

It is not fair.

Yes, I know that is the cry of a child. I do know the world is not fair. But I also believe passionately that the world is what we make of it and I will not be denied what is my right.

Why did Jit give in so feebly?

Some time before we took the exams — that was the most extraordinary part of the whole farce, being told to study as usual, being told that we should take the exams — Jit told me that she had made her choice of suitor. Out of the three, she had chosen Sobha Singh, another distant cousin, who was coming from Punjab to be married. One of the reasons why the weddings were to be in late

July was to give Sobha sufficient time for his papers to come through. Everything was arranged. Once he had arrived and they had met he would be found a job to tide him over while he perfected his English.

'Oh, I hope he speaks some English,' said Jit. 'Just think of the awfulness of the wedding night if he doesn't?'

Just think of the wedding night when Resham tells me this is only a marriage of convenience, I thought, but did not say.

Hetty and Megan eyed each other with frank admiration when Hetty got out of her car to meet the girl at her home. Hetty was so awed by the girl's shocking pink ensemble that she had not noticed Tom strolling round the corner of the cottage to see them off.

'Don't you both scrub up well,' he said approvingly.

'Thanks, Dad,' said Megan, preening.

Hetty was trying very hard not to flush with the unaccustomed praise.

Both of them had chosen to wear trouser suits — Hetty's was a plain deep blue — and whereas Megan's flowing tunic was covered with splodges of lime-green flowers, Hetty was wearing an easy jacket under which was a fashionably sparkling chemise. The sales assistant had been very persuasive and Hetty

90

was still amazed that not only had she fallen for the sales talk but she was actually wearing the garment.

'I thought no hat,' Hetty said tentatively. 'I've brought a scarf to cover my head.'

'Good thinking, so've I. I had meant to warn you. So let's go,' said Megan impatiently, 'or we'll be late.'

They arrived at the *Gurdwara* in excellent time, having found a nearby car park with spaces. The *Gurdwara* was a two-storeyed house in a predominantly Sikh area and apart from a neighbour of Balbiro's, they were the only non-Asians present. However, Jit had asked one of her extended family, a married cousin called Shamuna, to look after them. With a month-old baby on her hip, Shamuna was all smiles as she showed the two where to leave their shoes before she escorted them across the room to meet the brides.

The whole of what had originally been the living area of the 1920s house had been converted into one large room with the chimney and fireplace isolated in the centre. The walls were decorated with religious pictures and the floors were covered with carpets, some with beautifully muted hues and of venerable age. At one end of the room was the altar, dressed in a green silk cloth over a yellow cover on which lay the Holy

Book, the *Guru Granth Sahib*. Over the altar was a canopy suspended from the ceiling, of cloth of gold, red and green weave decorated with ribbons, and in front of the altar were vases of gladioli.

The women guests were no less magnificent, the effect rainbow-hued, a kaleidoscope of every colour imaginable, and amongst them Jit and Balbiro sat side by side on the floor surrounded by the chattering women. The brides were dressed almost identically, in red tunics embroidered in gold over red *shalwars*, and round each girl's shoulders was a red velvet scarf, while draped over their heads so that their faces were almost obscured were flimsy red veils.

'How splendid you both are!' Hetty's delight was so obvious that the women surrounding them beamed at her and applauded.

'Oh, but you must admire their jewellery,' said the neighbour, now introduced as Mrs Cooper, a large woman who looked as though once she was on the floor she would never be able to rise. 'Do show her, girls.'

The girl nearest Megan pulled aside her scarf and veil and the flushed face of Jit, shyly accepting the complimentary oohs and aahs of appreciation, smiled up at them. Jit held out her arms and Hetty and Megan admired

92

the rows of bangles and the rings and the necklaces all of gold, which glittered in the shaft of sunlight that fell across the room.

'Balbiro has the same as me,' said Jit. There was pride in her voice.

Balbiro remained silent. Hetty bent forward to touch Balbiro's hands, which lay listlessly on her trousered lap. They were icy cold and trembled slightly in her warm clasp.

'Balbiro, are you unwell? You're not going to be sick?' Hetty whispered urgently, her years of dealing with panic-stricken teenagers overcoming any reticence that a guest might be expected to feel.

Through the thin veil she could just make out a quiver of the girl's lips as Balbiro shook her head. Hetty felt a qualm of anxiety but her sense of place overrode it.

There was a stir round the door at the side of the room where the men were congregating. Jit hastily rearranged her veils so that she was completely covered once more as into the room came six young men.

'That's Keval, with the blue turban.' Mrs Cooper nudged Hetty's arm. 'He's Balbiro's brother. On his right with the pink turban and the garland is Resham, Balbiro's betrothed. I've seen him before: a polite young man, he is. And on Keval's left, wearing the gold turban must be their cousin,

Sobha, from India. I'm glad they're in traditional dress. I'd heard that Resham was intending to cut his hair.'

There was an intake of breath beside them. 'I'm sure that is not so,' one of the older women guests said stiffly. 'It would be outrageous.'

'I'm afraid I know little about Sikh traditions,' Hetty said apologetically, 'but I do know that not cutting his hair is very important to a man.'

'The last of our Sikh Gurus, Govind Singh, instituted the five symbols of our religion,' the woman said. 'Let me tell you about them. They are the *kara*, originally a sharp-edged quoit, now worn as a steel bangle; a symbol of restraint and a link to the Guru and also a symbol that God has no beginning nor end. There is the *kirpan*, which can be anything from three inches to three feet. It is kept in a sheath and may be worn over or under outer clothing. It symbolizes spirituality and defence of good and the weak. *Kachha* is the cotton underwear, a symbol of chastity.'

'They used to be cotton breeches which were suitable for riding in,' said Megan in an undertone.

'*Kesh* is the uncut hair which is twisted and knotted and held by the *kanga*, the wooden comb, symbolizing a clean mind and body,' continued their informant, smiling at Megan. 'And before you ask, a woman may not cut her body hair, either. Not even to trim her eyebrows. It is said that a Sikh should only bow his head to the Guru, not to a barber. So it is that if a man does not accept all of these he is no true follower.'

'Thank you for explaining it to me,' said Hetty sincerely. 'I am sure the girls' fathers have chosen well for them.'

Sobha was another handsome Indian, though looking less than comfortable in a suit that did not quite fit. The Singhs would change that soon enough, Hetty thought, though she was remembering dismally that Jit had expected so much more from her life than a marriage quite so soon after she left school. How young the bridegrooms looked, she reflected. Out of the corner of her eye she could see Balbiro shaking violently. Again she put out a tentative hand and touched her. The girl seemed to make an enormous effort; her whole body trembled once more, and was still.

'I hope Balbiro isn't going to throw up,' whispered Mrs Cooper, having heaved herself to her feet, with assistance, and now standing up next to Hetty. 'She didn't look at all well this morning. You should just see her face, under all that material.'

There was a harmonium being played, accompanied by a man on a small drum and a young boy who was shaking two rods of tiny cymbals. An elderly Sikh acting as priest began chanting prayers to which those present responded. Then Manjit and Balbiro's mother, Jasleen Kaur — whom Hetty had yet to meet — took their daughters by their hands and led them to the front of the canopy, where each girl knelt by the left side of her betrothed.

Shamuna, between Hetty and Megan, whispered, 'The Sikh marriage emphasizes the joining of two minds and two souls. A great deal of thought goes into matching a man and a woman because it is so important for them to live together in harmony. You see the bridegrooms are each carrying a white towel? These they were given at the time of their betrothal. The towels symbolize purity. In them are wrapped pieces of coconut which were given for a blessing. A heavy towel signifies the burden of worldly things, which the man will be called upon to carry during his marriage.'

The two couples stood up and made a circuit of the canopy, the bridegrooms carrying their white towels, the brides with their heads modestly lowered. The guests showered them with rose petals, Shamuna hastily thrusting handfuls towards Hetty and Megan, who joined in with gusto. There was a tense expectancy in the air.

'Four times they make the circle.' The woman who had explained the Sikh traditions turned to Hetty and Megan. 'Aah.' Her expelled sigh of relief was shared by everyone as, at the same moment, both girls caught hold of the free end of the towel her betrothed carried. 'Now they are married,' she said, 'for we believe that the wife shares the husband's burden, which the love of God makes as nothing.'

'A marriage of two minds. I like that,' said Hetty. Inwardly she was thinking that it required a great deal of forbearance on the part of a young man, and a great deal of courage from an inexperienced and possibly frightened girl. It was very different from the Western tradition. Yet maybe there was more support from the families joined together by an arranged marriage, who had more face to lose if things went wrong.

There was more joyous singing and the relatives went forward in turn to circle the bowed heads of the newly married couples with paper money. Then they laid the notes on the floor in front of them, a heap of red and purple and the occasional pink.

As she watched, enthralled, Hetty could

not help a small sigh. She could not doubt now that after such careful planning, Jit would find the happiness she sought in her marriage. But what of Balbiro? Had her trembling been more than simple nerves? Then Hetty intercepted a profound look that passed between Resham and his parents. There was pride in Harjot, the father for his son, a joyful acceptance of her new daughter-in-law by Resham's mother, Amita. There was no doubting that this bridegroom had found the bride he desired.

'They will be all right,' she whispered to Megan. 'Just see how happy Resham and his parents are.'

★ ★ ★

The ceremony was over. Megan was still inside, talking to one of the younger women. Hetty was lingering in the tiny front garden hoping to see Balbir Singh to thank him for inviting her to the ceremony and also to ask him to persuade Sobha to permit her to visit Jit occasionally. She knew this would not happen without permission.

Suddenly voices were raised in altercation. At first Hetty could not understand what was being said, but the angry tones of both men and women grew louder and, like a tide of colour, a wave of movement sent those in the garden back into the house to find out what was going on.

'What do you think is happening?' Hetty asked Megan anxiously. 'Do you think we should leave?'

'You are joking? I mean . . . leave now?'

A group of furious men, two red-clad figures clinging together in their midst, shouldered their way through the throng which followed them into the garden, perforce Hetty and Megan with them.

'Slut! Whore!' In a momentary cessation of noise, the words emerged with shocking clarity.

'It isn't true!' a female voice rang out. 'It didn't happen like that!'

There was another surge of movement and the blue-turbaned Keval dragged the brides apart, thrusting one into a waiting car.

'My husband, you cannot permit this to happen. Oh my God, this is not possible.'

Manjit Singh, who had followed closely behind the men, clutched the sleeve of her husband, Balbir, who threw her off irritably, his face suffused with a myriad of emotions, embarrassment and fury uppermost.

Manjit's face was streaming with tears that were no longer joyful as she clutched the girl who had been left behind to her bosom. The wave of agitated movement around them became a tumult of coloured silks, turbaned heads, muttering voices, heated, apprehensive faces.

Gradually the *Gurdwara* emptied and the guests slowly drifted away in small, gesticulating groups. It was over. The marriages had taken place, but something dire had occurred. The woman who had interpreted the ceremony for Hetty and Megan noticed that they were still in the garden. She hesitated, then came over, twisting a fold of her scarf in her fingers.

'Please,' Hetty began, 'would you tell us what is the matter? It is none of our business, I know. Only . . . we can see that something has happened concerning the brides.'

'Oh, it is dreadful!' wailed the woman, flushing scarlet, as if released from discretion. She turned her face away from the few wedding guests who remained. 'Dreadful . . . quite dreadful.'

'What has happened? Please tell us,' urged Megan.

'You see, when it was over, someone told someone else that she had heard Balbiro had run away from home. No. I cannot tell you.'

'I don't believe it,' said Megan loudly, her face ashen.

'Megan,' Hetty protested quietly. 'But

surely Balbiro wouldn't disgrace her family so. And why should this affect Jit?'

The woman lowered her voice. 'They said she couldn't be a virgin because of that. If it is true her husband will not take her. Her brother, Keval, has driven her home. It is so shameful. That it was said now. Her cousin, Jit, is shamed. We are all shamed. The whole Sikh community. Not a virgin. Oh, it is appalling. I must go,' she ended abruptly. 'My husband . . . ' She made a gesture of dismissal and left them.

'I think we'd better go, too,' said Hetty quietly, and without another word between them they returned to the car. What was there to say? But after a while Hetty asked, 'Are you all right, Megan?', concerned as she realized how pale the girl was. 'Megan?' The girl shrugged silently. 'I don't think there is anything we could do to help, do you? Not realistically, that is. We are strangers. The family would think it intrusive.'

'They are my friends.'

'And I have come to know Jit quite well in the sixth form. Nevertheless, this has to be a family matter.'

'Whatever.'

Hetty suppressed annoyance. 'Suppose you tell me what you think we should do.'

Megan turned her face away. 'Go home, I guess.'

So Hetty drove back to Otterhaven.

★   ★   ★

They had not eaten a thing, except for a chocolate bar, which Hetty said was in the glove compartment and which Megan declined — the only word she spoke during the entire journey — but Hetty could not face a convivial evening, which was bound to turn into a farce. When Tom urged her to join them for a meal she refused, saying she thought she'd just have a bath and an early bed.

'I'll ring you tomorrow,' said Tom.

Hetty could see concern in his face and realized, belatedly, that it was for her as well as for his daughter, who was still being non-communicative. 'I think I'll be going to church in the morning,' she said doggedly.

'Then I'll ring at lunchtime,' he persisted.

Hetty shrugged. Then she realized that she was behaving in the same way as his adolescent daughter and smiled for the first time since the traumatic events of the weddings. 'Thank you,' she said. 'I'll talk to you then.'

As she sat in the far from comfortable pew

in church the next day, Hetty thought to herself, What on earth am I doing here? It was the first time she had entered the building since her mother's funeral. Not that she was experiencing macabre sentiments or even feeling particularly doleful. Was it a seminal moment or merely an aberration? She did not know.

To make matters worse, it was a lovely sunny morning and a walk in the Brecon Beacons would have been much more to her taste. The views would be magnificent in the clear air. But she had said she would be home to take a call from Tom. It would have been so impolite not to be there.

Besides, to tell the truth, Hetty was as worried about Megan as she was about Jit and Balbiro. It was so unlike Megan not to chatter. Hetty had fully expected an in-depth exposition about the mechanics of the ceremony they had witnessed if not Megan's own opinions about arranged marriages. When it had gone so disastrously wrong, Hetty thought they would both speculate as to the whys and wherefores. Silence was disconcerting.

'How are you, Hetty? Such a long time since I've seen you.' It was Laura Blackstone, dressed in a flowered skirt and a tailored yellow linen jacket with an elaborate brooch pinned to her lapel, a gold vase with multi-coloured flowers and green leaves spilling out of it.

'Hello, Mrs Blackstone.' Hetty was in her blue trouser suit, this time with a plain white T-shirt. 'I'm very well. How are you?'

There followed a long description of Laura Blackstone's gall bladder, which was playing her up, ending, 'That is what old age brings — you wait and see.'

'I do hope not.'

'Then Joan had perfect health. So we thought.'

There was not much Hetty could think of to reply to this.

'And how are you spending your holidays? Such a long time you teachers have.' Too long was implied. Mr Blackstone had been an impoverished solicitor. Joan had never had much opinion of Laura's husband who, it was well known, was impoverished because of his penchant for the horses.

'I've spent a few days on Mull. Now I have to start work on next term's curriculum.'

'Of course. I suppose you wouldn't be able to help with the flowers next week?'

'The church flowers? I thought we'd established I had no talent.'

'It's time we want, not necessarily talent.'

Hetty could not prevent a look of

104

astonishment from crossing her face.

'Quite so. Well, you know what I mean.' Laura Blackstone actually looked flustered.

'As it happens, my Saturday mornings are likely to be taken up with The Grange.'

'The Beresfords' place? Ah.' There was a world of meaning in her voice. 'Clive Makepeace is such a charmer, isn't he?'

'Yes. Well, I suppose so. I've only met him once.'

'Well, good for you,' Laura said, not specifying what was so commendable. 'Anyway, don't be a stranger, will you?'

The vicar shook her hand warmly. 'The first time after a funeral is always the worst.'

'I'm usually busy on a Sunday morning.' Hetty was determined that this visit should be seen as an aberration rather than a precedent.

'We do a choral evensong once a month,' said the vicar determinedly. 'It's very popular.'

Hetty made her escape.

Tom rang while she was grilling a small chop.

'Did you sleep well?' There was a pause, then a chuckle sounded down the line. 'I really mean that. I found Megan drinking coffee at three o'clock this morning.'

'That wouldn't have helped.'

'No, she's still asleep.'

There was another pause. Hetty was about to say that she had slept quite well, considering, when Tom continued, 'There is something bothering her. I'd like your advice.'

'I expect it is just the shock of what happened yesterday.'

'No, it's more than that. I'm quite sure about it.'

She did not want to get involved. She did not want to get *more* involved than she was already. Hetty said, 'I've a lot of work to do. That's why I went to church this morning instead of walking.'

'You don't want to get involved.'

'It's not that,' she said indignantly.

'Of course not.' His voice took on a cold timbre. 'I'm sorry I bothered you. I quite understand. Goodbye, Hetty.'

'But . . . '. Quietly but inexorably the phone had been put down.

Tears came into Hetty's eyes. She blew her nose violently. She was not going to weep. It was almost as if she were menopausal. The thought brought a flush to her body. Irritatedly, she threw off the cardigan she had put on over her T-shirt. Not again. Heated flesh was such a bore. She sniffed. As if to mock her, the odour of burning flesh wafted into the sitting-room where the landline was. Drat and double drat. It was her chop. Hetty turned off the grill, rescued the pan and thrust it into the sink. Then she burst into tears.

After she had recovered sufficiently to make herself a cheese sandwich, Hetty thought once more about Tom's phone call. She had been very aloof. Not in the least friendly, considering that what he was asking from her was comparatively little. Just some advice about his daughter, he had said. Would that have been so very much?

Hetty did not want to be involved.

'But I am involved already,' she said aloud. She had taken Megan to see Jit. It was because of that visit that the two of them had received their invitations to the weddings. She had met Tom in Mull (Best forget what happened on Iona.) She had been at the wedding ceremony. She knew, without anyone telling her, that Megan was more upset than — whatever it was that had happened — was warranted.

Hetty found the number and lifted the receiver. Suppose Tom had already asked for someone else's help? How humiliating it would be when he told her she needn't bother. There was no need to submit herself to that. Was there?

'I'm sorry,' she said without any preamble, without even asking to speak to him, when the phone was picked up. 'That was unpardonable of me. What can I do?'

'I'd just like to talk.' His voice was neutral.

'Without Megan?' He had not forgiven her. Hetty persisted bravely.

After a moment Tom said, 'I'd prefer to come to your house.' But his tone was warmer. 'There is a reason.'

Hetty took a deep breath. 'I've just ruined my chop. There's nothing else to eat in the house. I'd intended doing a supermarket shop tomorrow. Suppose I buy something for dinner tonight, for the two of us? I mean, I'm not much of a cook but I can do pasta.'

'Thank you. Hetty, I really don't know how to handle this. This thing with Megan, I mean.'

'I'm not sure why you have any faith in me,' she replied frankly, 'especially after that exhibition of lack of neighbourliness. But I will try.'

Hetty was not sure, but she thought she heard another chuckle just before she put down the receiver.

# 6

Tom arrived promptly for dinner. The first thing he did when he stepped over Hetty's threshold was to sniff the air appreciatively. 'Lovely smell of garlic,' he said, putting down a parcel by the hall table.

'I never thought to ask first if you like it,' said Hetty, thinking it was just as well that the smell of burning chop had gone. 'It's just a very plain spaghetti bolognese, otherwise.'

'I use garlic a lot when I cook.'

'It's such a warm evening I've laid a table outside. Is that all right?'

'Hetty. Stop sounding so apologetic,' Tom said impatiently. 'We had a difference of opinion. Friends are entitled to fall out, you know.'

'Provided they make up?'

'Exactly so. Now, I didn't bring wine because I wasn't sure what you were cooking. Would you like me to go round the corner for something?'

'I've white wine in the fridge or red in the kitchen. Which would you prefer?'

'Let's open the red.'

The front door opened into a miniscule

hallway. Hetty led Tom through the hall and into the sitting-room. 'I'll fetch the wine.'

The sitting-room was a generous size with French windows leading into the garden. Tom could see a garden table covered by a leaf-patterned cloth and already laid for their meal just outside the windows. There were plain green cushions on two of the white metal chairs. The garden was small and walled and paved with old flagstones. There were one or two raised beds and a few shrubs. It was south facing and would be hot in the middle of the day, though now it was cool and leafy and fragrant with the scent of jasmine, which was drifting into the room. Tom moved towards the doors but was arrested by the sight of his painting over the mantelpiece. He was regarding it critically when Hetty returned with the wine and two glasses.

'Will you open it?' she asked.

'I'm honoured.' He took the tray from her and nodded towards the painting. 'Most people put my stuff in a corner.'

'That I don't believe.'

'Well, I hope that isn't entirely true.' He busied himself with the corkscrew. 'The thing is, now that you've already hung one of my paintings I feel a bit embarrassed — '

'Whatever for?' she interrupted.

He passed her a glass of wine. 'I left it in the hall. Just a minute.' He returned with a small parcel wrapped in brown paper. 'A peace offering.'

'Oh,' said Hetty. 'I thought that was my job.'

'Dinner,' he said. 'That's yours. Aren't you going to open it?'

'Of course. Ohh,' said Hetty, as she allowed the brown paper to drop to the floor. It was a framed watercolour of the beach on Iona. Hetty recognized it immediately. There was a woman on the beach, looking out to sea. It was her.

'I don't usually do people,' said Tom diffidently. 'But the beach seemed to cry out for some human interest. I suppose it could be anyone, if you don't like the idea of being an artist's model.'

'You remembered what I was wearing.'

'Just some cotton trousers and a shirt.'

'Well, you remembered the exact colour. I-I'm very flattered. Would it be too presumptuous to put it over the mantelpiece instead of the Blorange?'

'Not if you really like it.'

'I do,' she said simply. 'Thank you, Tom.'

There was a pause. It was not in the least awkward. 'I've fixed the wire ready for it to be hung,' he said at last, dragging his eyes from

111

her face. 'Would you like me to do that for you?'

His eyes were dark, unfathomable. She lowered hers with difficulty. Then, belatedly, she nodded in agreement, so he took down the picture of the Blorange and hung the new one in its place.

'Just a little more to the left,' she said, feeling calmer, standing back and assessing the angle critically. 'I can't bear crooked pictures.'

'Nor I. Is that better? Great. Hetty, what was there before?'

'A singularly depressing print of the churchyard. Mother admired it a lot but I loathed it.'

He smiled. 'Then I hope you have pleasure in this. You know, I'd really like to paint you properly, one day. Do you think you'd sit for me? Though I warn you, my portraits aren't as good as my views.'

Sit for him! Hetty flushed. This flush was different. Instead of making her remember her age it made her feel like a young girl. Then she said primly, 'Provided I keep all my clothes on.'

He grinned. 'Hetty, you're flirting.'

'I'm not. I . . . ' She thought, Maybe I am. She changed the subject abruptly. 'Tom, do you want to talk, or eat first?'

112

'Eat first, if that is all right? I'm still not sure about . . . Let's go into the garden, anyway. It looks great out there.'

'Please don't examine it too closely. My mother was the gardener, not I.' She could see a sudden frown cross his face. 'I know what you're going to say. My mother did the cooking, she did the gardening. You want to know what was my part in all this.'

'Actually, I was merely going to ask you why you always denigrate yourself. You do, you know,' he insisted gently, as Hetty opened her mouth to deny it. 'You put yourself down all the time.'

'Only over things like my cooking and my lack of knowledge of gardening,' she protested. She went on determinedly, 'I'm a very good teacher. I have an excellent rapport with my students.'

'Which is why I'm here.'

'I have an excellent sense of self-esteem. I'll fetch the food,' she said.

'Another of the reasons why I'm here.' He took hold of her arm as she made to pass him. 'Let me carry something.'

Hetty shook off his hand, saying crossly, 'I don't know why I said that. I don't know why it is you always make me utter something stupid.'

'Other than denigrating yourself, I've never

heard you say anything remotely stupid.'

Tom's protestation sounded as though he really meant it. The trouble was, Hetty thought, as she watched him pour wine for himself and raise his glass to her, that she was not used to dealing with men — a man — on any level other than the strictly professional one at school. Half the time she was not sure what it was Tom wanted from her, though that was wrong in this instance for he had already told her that what he wanted was help over the thing that was troubling his daughter.

'It is a most peculiar effect you have on me, do you realize that, Tom Gillard?'

'I'm beginning to.' He sounded, if anything, complacent. 'Though the immediate answer to that is that I'm starving. Come on, let's eat.'

The meal progressed amicably. There was a good, green salad. 'Herbs from the garden. I do know about those.' There was a bowl of cherries to follow. 'I hope you've had enough to eat tonight. I'm not used to male appetites. Coffee?'

'At my age,' said Tom solemnly, 'you tend not to overeat.'

Hetty looked at him. They both laughed. 'Coffee? I forgot. You prefer herbal tea.'

'I'd rather have another glass of wine.'

'That I can manage.' She shivered. 'Shall we go inside? This isn't, after all, the Mediterranean.'

They settled themselves comfortably with a coffee table between them, another bottle opened. A moth fluttered in through the open door and settled near the lamp by Tom's chair, the only illumination in the room.

After a bit, Tom said, 'Will you give me your version of what happened yesterday?'

Hetty went through the day's events carefully.

'Megan didn't mention anything about Balbiro appearing unduly nervous,' he commented thoughtfully. 'It all came as such a shock to her she has hardly said a word, except to explain that you were home early because the whole event ended in a fiasco. Her silence, in itself, is enough to make me worried.'

Hetty remembered that Megan had been very quiet in the car; that she had been expecting a flood of speculation. She said so to Tom. 'I suppose it is just that she feels for the girls,' she ended.

'That's lame.'

'So it is, but it's the best I can do. So I'm not sure how you want me to help you.'

'I have this strange feeling that somehow Megan is involved.'

'Involved! How could Megan possibly be involved in any of this?'

'That is what I should like you to help me find out.'

'I can't.'

'Why can't you?' Tom leant forward to pour some more wine into Hetty's glass.

Hetty, who usually drank very circumspectly, hardly realized what he was doing. She said, 'How on earth can I find out if Megan had anything to do with what happened yesterday?'

'By asking her.'

'I couldn't do that. Besides, she is far more likely to tell you than she would be if I tried to interfere.'

'The fact is you don't want to become implicated with any of this.'

'That's not true. I just don't see . . . ' Hetty stopped. Why should she become caught up in affairs that were not her problem and definitely none of her making? As if her life hadn't become complicated enough, with her mother's affairs to settle. It was true that she was already concerned about the three girls and since the beginning of the summer she had become particularly fond of Megan. On occasions she had actually wondered if they might become friends, despite the disparity in their ages.

'It really isn't any business of ours, or Megan's, if it comes to that,' she persisted all the same.

'Then you should say so. Believe me, I did try. It was as if I hadn't spoken. Maybe if you tell her it isn't our business she will be less bothered about it.'

In-depth talks with her father would be one of Megan's problems. Not having a mother figure in her childhood must have been very traumatic for the girl, Hetty was thinking. Remembering Manjit Singh, an inkling of the fondness Megan had for the motherly woman came into her mind. It was no wonder Megan was so upset by the turn of events. She put down the wine glass without taking the sip she had intended drinking.

'Does Megan have a mother figure in her life?' she asked quietly.

'No. Though she is fond of my sister.' Tom did not pretend he misunderstood the question. 'I have been both mother and father to her. Nor have any girlfriends I may have had in the past taken any part in Megan's life. You see, I could never envisage any one of them becoming important enough for me to risk them having to upset her by making a sudden exit when our relationship soured.'

'I see.' Hetty could, indeed, understand his reasoning. So where did that leave her?

117

'You are different,' Tom said.

For a moment, Hetty was convinced she had spoken the question aloud. She was appalled. She picked up her wine glass and took a gulp.

'You are different because your relationship with my daughter pre-dates any relationship we might have.'

He was going far too fast for her. 'I'd like to think we are friends,' she said primly.

'So it is as a friend, and as my daughter's teacher, that I am asking you to become involved in this bit of bother which is worrying her. Will you? Please, Hetty.'

He had done it so adroitly. There was no way out of this. Hetty sensed that she was being manipulated like a puppet in the hands of a master. If she refused, she knew that whatever Tom might have meant about a relationship, he would cut her out of his life without a qualm. He had already admitted to a certain ruthlessness with other women. There would be no more little dinners; the voluntary gardening job would probably have to go to save them both awkwardness. He might even take back his painting of Iona. She thought, I am becoming a selfish cow. All Tom is asking me to do is to try to discover exactly why Megan is apparently so upset.

'I suppose Megan might even like to talk to

118

me, since I was there, once she has got over the initial shock,' she said at last, hesitantly.

'Precisely. Hetty, thank you. I hate to see her like this and I know that whatever I said to her wouldn't make any difference. Would you be able to come over tomorrow?'

'Tomorrow? Why, yes, I suppose so.'

They agreed that Hetty would come for tea. It would seem less formal than if she were asked for a meal. 'Besides, I have work to do. I can't just drop that because of a whim,' Tom declared.

'And if we leave it another day, I expect Megan will be feeling much better about the whole thing,' Hetty agreed.

Shortly afterwards he took his leave, getting up and saying how much he had enjoyed her company. At the front door, he took both her hands in his and squeezed them gently.

'Thank you for a lovely dinner, Hetty, and for listening to me. I begin to think that daughters in their late teens are more of a headache than when it was all slammed doors and histrionics.'

Feeling unthreatened and entirely sympathetic, Hetty smiled back, leaving her hands in his. 'From what I have heard from other parents there could be worse to come, though Megan has always struck me as being a very solicitous young woman, which is why she

119

and Jit have been such good friends.'

'That's what worries me,' he said, seriously. He bent down towards her and kissed her on the cheek. 'See you for tea, Hetty.'

She was left in a confused and more than a little apprehensive state. That night the words 'relationship' and 'involvement' rolled round her brain. She knew it was the wine but feared that the man, himself, was a not inconsiderable part of her concern.

Balbiro's Journal, 3rd July

I ran away.

It was after the exams. I'd thought and thought about it and when I was so sure Resham didn't really want to marry me, that he was being forced into this just as much as me, I ran away.

They say that if you sway with the wind it does not destroy you. This wind felt like a monstrous storm. My heart was breaking. In sheer self-preservation I had to rebel.

I thought about it carefully. I decided that I would take as much money as I could get together and catch a bus to Birmingham. I would buy English clothes from a charity shop so that no one would recognize me, then I would find a room in a woman's refuge. You see? I was not so stupid as to think I could manage this all on my own. Then I intended to get a job. After that? It remained to be seen.

But you know what? The obstacle that was in the way of my freedom was the lack of money. I've never really had any money of my own except for a few pounds to spend on something personal. During my preparation I managed to scrape together some £50. I'll not say how. It was because of the money that I knew how unrealistic I was being. £50 would get me nowhere.

Then I remembered Megan — the only English girl I've ever really known. Without involving Jit because of the trouble it would cause, I told Megan everything. She agreed with me that the money was insufficient. She offered to lend me £100 — which I thought was pretty generous. It came with a catch. She insisted that instead of running away to Birmingham straight away I should go home with her first.

Her father was away, she said. I would be quite safe. From there we could make plans together.

What a fool. I should have known she would try to talk me out of it. It was a betrayal.

No, I don't believe that Megan set out to betray me. She never knew that her father had persuaded her brother to go home to see her.

I liked Jake. He was the first English boy I had talked to — without an adult being present. But Jake was worried on my account, like his sister. They both tried to talk me out of the mess I had got myself into. Jake even suggested that I should

121

telephone Resham and ask him how he really felt about our marriage.

I couldn't do that. I mean . . .

So in the end I allowed myself to be persuaded.

I phoned Jit and told her what had happened and Jake took Megan and me to Chepstow. Jit really surprised me giving in to her parents as she had. I thought she had more guts. But no, it seemed that she was already half in love with Sobha (With the idea of Sobha??)

Then Jit and I got the bus to Bristol and she came home with me. I suppose that was kind of her because she was going to get into trouble with my parents, let alone her own, but I swore she had nothing to do with the running away and my father grunted and huffed but rang Uncle Balbir who came to fetch her.

Of course I knew what would happen once Jit had gone home.

This time my father beat me. It was bad, like nothing I had ever imagined. Even my mother was shocked. She cried out to him to stop, and when he wouldn't she yelled that he mustn't leave a mark.

There is a small scar on my shoulder, where I bled. I think it might fade in time.

Two days after the beating I told them that I would marry Resham.

I mean, what else was I supposed to do?

Hetty spent Monday morning doing a load of washing and generally cleaning the house. She wondered how she was going to cope with the household chores once term started again. She had always done more than her share of the housework but in general Joan had shopped and cooked for them both. Maybe finding a housekeeper would be a good idea. She could afford it, and she was beginning to think that shutting herself away would be far from sensible. Having to forego the gardening job on a Saturday morning for mere housework would be risible.

Over a salad lunch she went through her wardrobe mentally, and sighed. Why were her clothes so dull? She had absolutely nothing to wear for tea with the Gillards. How facile, she chided herself. She was hardly being invited over for a garden party. It had cooled down since the weekend and her denim skirt with a Liberty print short-sleeved shirt would do very well. But a few new things for the autumn might be fun to buy. She might even find someone to go shopping with for a little advice. Vera was always well dressed, if in a somewhat outlandish way. Not that she wanted to emulate her mother's generation, with their pleated skirts and good jackets. Also, Vera was her own age and asking the advice of someone younger — Megan?

— might result in mutton dressed as lamb. Hetty winced. That would be just so humiliating.

She arrived at the cottage on Gaer Hill at the appointed time, wearing her denim skirt, bare-legged with canvas shoes but also carrying a blue cotton cardigan in case it became chilly. She parked the car neatly and found Tom waiting for her in the front garden, dead-heading roses.

'I've only just told Megan you were coming,' he said.

Hetty had wondered if Megan, sensing that her father was worried about her, might have contrived a way of escaping from her parent for the day. But the girl, having spent the greater part of the morning in bed, was now sitting under a tree with a book in her hand.

'I've made cucumber sandwiches,' said Tom, as he settled Hetty next to Megan. 'Earl Grey or Assam, Hetty?'

'I'd love some Earl Grey, if there's lemon.'

'Earl Grey it is. Megan?'

'Thanks, Dad.'

'No 'I'll get it for you, Dad', then. Never mind — you may do the washing up. I'll be back in a minute.'

Hetty sat in one of the two extra chairs Tom had produced and adjusted the cushion behind her back, wondering how she was going to broach the subject of the weddings. How long was Tom going to be, for a start? Should she . . . ?

'I suppose you are here to quiz me about Balbiro.'

'Excuse me?'

'Dad won't be out for ages. He obviously wants to give us time alone. You may have noticed he's not the most subtle of men.'

Hetty looked at Megan and smiled. 'You are very fond of your father, aren't you?'

'Of course I am. Dad's great as far as fathers go, but that doesn't mean I can't see his faults.'

'I suppose not.' In her opinion Tom was a very complex man but she thought this was not quite the sort of thing one told a man's daughter. Moreover, this was not the way in which Hetty had imagined the conversation would proceed at all. There was a moment's silence while in her mind she attempted several versions of what she had planned to say.

'It was dreadful, on Saturday, wasn't it?' Megan broke into her thoughts, putting down her book with a thud.

Automatically Hetty registered that Megan was reading *The Life of Pi*. She would far rather have initiated a discussion on the book but instead she answered quietly, 'I can't get

Saturday out of my mind. Do you remember exactly what it was we were told?'

'Some old biddy told someone else that Balbiro wasn't a virgin. I mean, get real. Are they living in the dark ages, or what?'

'But it's not like that, is it, Megan? You know that from how we've discussed it at school. It most definitely is not like that for Asian girls. It's one of the reasons they marry comparatively young. Why am I telling you this? Being such friends with Jit and Balbiro and their families you must know more about their beliefs and traditions than I do.'

'Maybe. It's barbaric, all the same.'

'Look, the whys and wherefores are not at issue here,' Hetty said firmly. 'But that Balbiro is suspected of no longer being a virgin is what I understood. Someone had accused Balbiro of running away from home. Because of that it was assumed that she could no longer be a virgin. If that is found to be the case, her husband has the right to repudiate her without any repercussions. That's the way it is.'

'They can't know, and anyway, now that she is married, what difference does it make?'

'Megan, I can't believe that you still don't appreciate the implications for an Asian girl. And of course they can find out.'

'By dragging her to a doctor, I suppose.'

'Precisely, and please don't make barbarity an issue. Whether you or I agree, it just is the way it is. But what I would very much like to know,' Hetty went on, determined not to allow the conversation to be sidetracked into a diatribe against the beliefs and customs of another culture, 'is why you are so upset about it all? Your father is very concerned about you.'

'Whatever.' The girl shrugged.

'Such a maddening response,' Hetty said calmly. 'Next question. What are you going to do about it?'

'What am I . . . ' Startled, Megan sat up. 'It's got nothing to do with me. Nothing.'

'That's what I thought,' said Hetty, 'but I am beginning to wonder. I mean, you are protesting most vehemently. You haven't speculated in any way, which seems suspicious to my mind — almost as though you know all about what happened.'

'That's not true!'

'Isn't it?'

'Will you pour, Megan, or shall I?' Tom had come up behind them, silently putting down the tea tray. 'Don't go, my darling.' He put a restraining hand on his daughter's arm, for she had risen to her feet lithely and it was obvious that she was about to storm off. 'I think, maybe, that Hetty is right and that you do know a little more about this than you are telling us. I don't mean that what happened wasn't unexpected but . . . '

'Oh, all right. Don't nag, don't push me. But it's not my fault and anyway, it's not true.'

'I'll pour,' said Hetty quietly. 'Sit down, Tom. Pass the sandwiches, Megan, then sit down and tell us what you do know.'

Resignedly, Megan did as she was told. Hetty sighed with relief for she had fully expected the girl to have flounced back into the cottage in a huff. Anger, either on the part of the outraged girl, or from her exasperated father, was never going to get to the bottom of this.

'When did you last see Jit?' Hetty asked. The answer surprised her.

'About two weeks ago.'

'But we visited her in Chepstow at the beginning of the holidays.'

'Why don't you just tell us what happened,' Tom prompted gently, helping himself to two more sandwiches and passing first Hetty then Megan the plate.

'I couldn't.' Megan pushed the plate away, though she sat down. 'Balbiro phoned me. She told me all about Resham and how she was in trouble with her family because she didn't want to marry him. She said she was going to run away. Balbiro had some stupid idea that she could find a woman's refuge, somewhere where she was unknown. But she needed help from me because she didn't want to involve Jit. I guess she knew that Jit would be in fearful trouble herself if it came out that she had helped her cousin run away. I wonder if she wasn't sure she could trust Jit to keep a secret?'

There was a pause while Megan pondered this. Tom and Hetty sat very still.

'Balbiro was going to get a job . . . '

'A job, what sort of a job?' Hetty interrupted. 'Balbiro's not qualified to do anything in particular.'

'I don't know. Waitressing. You don't need much experience to get a job doing that.'

'Not the point,' said Tom, quietly. 'Did Balbiro run away?'

'Yes,' Megan sighed. 'But she didn't run away to a woman's refuge. She came here.'

# 7

The news that Megan was directly implicated in that shocking scene outside the *Gurdwara* did not come as that much of a surprise to Hetty. As the afternoon had progressed she had already realized that the whole matter was far more serious than Tom Gillard imagined. Judging by his white, set expression, he was only just absorbing this possibility, only just beginning to calculate what it would mean.

'I think you'd better begin again, at the beginning,' he said grimly to his daughter, who had moved to sit sideways on her sun lounger with her shoulders slumped, the expression on her face one compounded of misery and defiance.

'It was entirely my idea,' Megan insisted eventually, when she had squirmed on her chair for a while, chewing the end of a lock of her long hair so that both Tom and Hetty were sure that not only did she regret what she had told them already but that she had intended to say nothing more. But instead she sighed deeply as she picked up her cup and saucer. Then, taking a deep breath, she went on to explain that she thought that Balbiro would not be able to cope on her own if she ran away to a totally strange place. 'She's not like us. I mean, neither Balbiro nor Jit have even been to Cardiff on their own, let alone Birmingham or London. Besides, she hadn't much money, either,' she told them, more at ease now that her story had been received without immediate condemnation. 'I don't think either of the girls ever had much spare cash, though they were always given what they wanted.' She bit her lip. 'I offered to lend her £100 from my savings account.'

'Oh, Meg, I doubt if you'd ever have seen it again.'

'Dad! That was the least of my worries. I thought I'd never see Balbiro again if I didn't help her.'

'It was very generous of you,' said Hetty quietly.

'I-I was frightened for her. I mean, you never know, nowadays, do you? All the papers tell you that the moment a girl is seen on the streets alone she is game for the sex traffickers.'

'Meg . . . ' her father expostulated weakly.

'It's true, though, isn't it, Dad?' Megan just knew Balbiro would be in terrible trouble with her family if she disappeared. Ranjit

Singh and Jasleen Kaur, Balbiro's parents, were very different from Balbir Singh and Manjit Kaur. Though Megan had been treated kindly by the Bristol Singhs on the occasions when she and Jit had visited Balbiro, she had gained the distinct impression that though they might not have anything against her personally, they disapproved of Jit's friendship with her. And they travelled from Chepstow to Bristol by bus! Alone! Balbiro was never allowed on public transport by herself. Her mother drove her to school each morning and collected her in the afternoon. (At least Balbiro's mother had a car to drive, but her family was probably better off than Jit's.)

'You see, I thought she could phone her mother when she got here,' Megan continued. 'To settle her mind. But Balbiro refused to do anything of the sort, so what could I do? I could hardly phone her family myself. Then, though I was really afraid about what might happen to her, I was sure that she would be found, wherever she went. Most Indian girls are found eventually, aren't they, if they run away? At least, that's what you see in the papers. I guessed there would be a lot of trouble about family honour and all that unless she was with a friend. I thought that if she came here she would have time to think,

132

space to decide whether she could stand being married, or if she really wanted to leave her family for good. At the time it all seemed so sensible.'

'Sensible . . . ' repeated her father faintly.

'It was a kind thought,' said Hetty.

'But idiotically altruistic,' snarled Tom, his forbearance stretched to breaking. 'You might have guessed it would end in a cock-up. If you really thought she needed breathing space, why didn't you just suggest to her family openly that she came to stay with you for a few days?'

'I didn't suggest it because I knew her family would refuse to allow her to come. I'm not that stupid.'

'Stupid enough to assist her to do the one thing that was guaranteed to make her family furious.'

'Balbiro was reluctant to come though she knew she would be quite safe here. I think it was the money that finally persuaded her,' Megan said sadly. 'She fully expected her family to come round to her way of thinking eventually. While she was here . . . '

'When was she here?' demanded her father suddenly.

'While you were in Scotland.'

Tom groaned. 'Please don't tell me it was the week when Jake was in this country.' He turned to Hetty. 'Jake is my son, Megan's brother.'

'Megan has mentioned him. Doesn't he work abroad?'

'He came home unexpectedly for a conference. We had a long chat on the phone before he flew over. I suggested he might like to see his sister as she was on her own in the cottage. You weren't though, were you?'

'There was only Balbiro here. We weren't having wild parties, if that's what you're implying. It was cool seeing him unexpectedly.'

'Nothing would be less acceptable to Balbiro's family than Megan's unmarried brother.'

'You are joking, I hope.'

'Hetty, I'm not sure that I am,' said Tom. 'So, Balbiro met Jake. What happened then?'

'Absolutely nothing. Jakey stayed for twenty-four hours. We didn't even eat out. But he could see that Balbiro was upset about something. I don't know, somehow she was persuaded to tell him that she was running away. He was very good with her, suggested that she might even try to get in touch with Resham herself and find out how he felt about the marriage. Balbiro said she couldn't do that. Then she seemed to come to a decision. She told us that she would go home.

She said that she'd probably agree to marry Resham, after all. She actually told me that she'd always fancied him so after that I didn't think there was anything to worry about.'

'Good Lord,' groaned Tom, running his hands through his hair.

'They'd known each other since primary school. Balbiro said that Resham used to pull her plaits.'

'From such small beginnings does romance spring,' said Hetty.

'Twaddle,' he muttered.

It was an aside that was perfectly audible to the two women. Involuntarily their eyes met and even through their common anxiety a glimmer of a sympathetic smile for the matter-of-factness of a mere male lit both their faces.

'Anyway, Balbiro decided that since Resham seemed to want to marry her, perhaps it wouldn't be as bad a thing as she'd imagined. So she said. So Jake and I took her to Chepstow where we met Jit, then they caught another bus to Bristol and Jit went home with her. Jit rang me afterwards. There had been an almighty row as I suppose they must have expected. But apparently Balbiro did tell her parents she'd marry Resham and Jit said the weddings were to take place as planned. You see, the weddings had not been cancelled or anything. No one else suspected anything. It shouldn't have happened like that. It's so unfair for it all to have gone wrong now.'

'The next question is, what happens now?' said Hetty.

'Not in doubt,' said Tom. 'Megan has to tell the families precisely what did occur and try to put things right.'

Megan went white. Hetty rescued the cup, which was rattling on its saucer and which the girl was still holding, setting them both down on the tray. Then she took Megan's hand and pressed it gently.

'Would you like me to come with you?' she asked quietly.

'I know I should go and see Balbiro, but I don't think I can.'

'It's not a question . . . ' he was silenced by Hetty's glance.

'Do you know Balbiro's family?' she asked.

'Obviously not as well as Jit's,' answered Megan.

She wondered if Keval would be there. She had never liked — never trusted — Keval. When she was thirteen and they had just met he ordered her about in the same way he lorded it over his sister; expecting services from the girls, like fetching and carrying, as though they were his personal servants. Then recently he had taken to looking through her as though she were dirt. Yet Jit had told her once that Keval used to go to nightclubs and had his first English girl when he was fifteen. Megan had been appalled though she could see how it would be: the girl would be flattered, intrigued, easily persuaded.

For herself, though she was on the aspirational list of many of the local boys, Megan had never gone the whole way with any of them. She was no longer a virgin, having had an experience with a cousin when she was only fifteen. It had not lasted. It could not have done, given that they saw each other only twice a year at most. It had not been in the least earth-shattering, very mundane, even. Innate caution or sufficient self-knowledge to understand she wasn't ready — one of the two had persuaded Megan to remain aloof. Possibly Jit's influence, with her very different take on life, had had a great deal to do with it.

'Perhaps it would be best if we talked to Jit's mother first,' Hetty said into Megan's reflective pause.

'Would you go with her, Hetty?' asked Tom, still visibly shaken. 'I'll drive you both to Chepstow, perhaps wait in the car while you go into the house . . . '

'Opting out, Dad?'

'Not in the least, but in the circumstances I think this is something for women to talk about. I'll speak to Balbiro's father, if I have to.'

That would not be a pleasant interview, Hetty thought. None of it was going to be pleasant. 'When do you think we should go?'

'I can't tomorrow,' said Tom. 'I have to go to Cardiff.'

'Wednesday isn't very convenient for me,' said Hetty hesitantly, reluctant to seem unhelpful but not happy with any of this. 'I don't think we should delay for too long but I do have an appointment with my solicitor. Of course, I could change it.'

'No, don't do that,' said Tom. 'We'll go to Chepstow on Thursday.'

'Should we telephone first?' asked Hetty.

'Much better not,' advised Megan unexpectedly. 'Manjit Kaur will remember a reason why it's not convenient. But she spends most of her time at home so we are unlikely to find her out.'

'So we'll pick you up about three o'clock on Thursday, Hetty?'

'That will be fine.' It would not be fine, naturally. Hetty was dreading the whole thing and probably wouldn't be able to sleep until it was all over. 'I think I'd better go,' she said. 'Thank you for tea.'

138

'Don't go yet,' said Tom. 'Stay a little longer.'

'I'll take the tray inside,' said Megan with commendable diplomacy. 'There's something I want to do.'

'Not phone Jit, I hope?'

'No, Dad, but I thought if I texted her and said I wanted to see her at home on Thursday she would make absolutely sure her mother is in.'

'But you don't know where Jit will be. She could be with her own husband by now. After all, the scandal, such as it is, doesn't touch her,' Hetty pointed out.

'Which is why texting is so useful,' said Megan patiently. 'After all, wherever she is, Jit is hardly likely to have had her mobile confiscated.'

With that she picked up the tray and walked back into the cottage.

There was a pause while the adults sat, crushed by teenage logic.

'Oh, Lord, I do hope she's right.'

'Do you think we should . . . '

'Go tomorrow? I've already said I can't. No, much better to leave it as we planned.'

'But it is our business, after all,' sighed Hetty.

'Not yours, ours.'

'But I was there. I heard it all.'

'I think we should drop the whole matter. At least for now. Else neither of us will sleep tonight.'

'I'd already thought of that. You know,' said Hetty, 'I think we should go right now. The whole set of circumstances are still fresh in Megan's mind. We all know that damage has been done. If we leave it, who knows if it can ever be repaired?'

'Why did I have the feeling you were going to come all noble on me?'

'I don't feel in the least noble. I'm terrified by the whole sequence of events,' replied Hetty.

'Even though you are not implicated?'

Hetty turned to see Tom smiling at her through the strain in his eyes. 'Will you tell Megan? I need the loo before we go.'

He was on his feet, ready to go inside. Then he said over his shoulder, 'I do like a woman who calls a spade a spade. The loo is on your left by the front door. We'll be ready in five minutes.'

★ ★ ★

No one said anything as Tom drove down the Wye Valley. The Singhs' cul-de-sac was quiet, tree-lined. Tom parked then, reaching into the back for the paper; said he'd stay for as long as it took.

'Come and fetch me immediately if Mr Singh wants to talk to me.'

Hetty and Megan walked up the drive together and Hetty rang the bell.

The door was opened by Jit. Gone were the jeans and the casual appearance of their previous meeting at her home. Jit was wearing *shalwar kameez* in a pretty green print. Behind her they could see a young man hovering. Hetty recognized him immediately as Sobha Singh, Jit's new husband. Unlike his wife, Sobha was wearing jeans and a white T-shirt with a navy blue turban.

Hetty felt an immediate surge of relief and hope. If Jit and Sobha were still together, there was a small chance that Balbiro was with Resham. If so, they could all go straight home and consider the incident over.

'What are you doing here, Meg, Miss Loveridge? I thought you weren't coming until Thursday.'

'Hello, Jit,' said Hetty. 'I hope it won't be too inconvenient to see your mother this afternoon. You're right. We had intended to come on Thursday, but when we thought about it, we decided we shouldn't wait.'

'Who this?' demanded the young man, pushing forward.

Heavens, and he doesn't even have much

141

English, thought Hetty.

'This is Miss Loveridge. She is my teacher,' said Jit, clearly and slowly. 'You know, teacher, school?'

'Ah. Teacher. I know teacher.'

'And Megan, Megan is my friend. She was at the wedding.' Sobha Singh smiled, then he frowned as he recalled the circumstances of the wedding and had the wit to recognize trouble on the doorstep.

'I'll see if my mother is available.'

Hetty said, 'Please, Jit. It is very important. We should like to talk to you and your mother. Now.'

'You'd better come in,' replied the girl reluctantly. She showed them into the same front room where they had been before. Her husband made to accompany them but she turned him round and pushed him back into the hall. 'They see just Ma and me. Please.'

The two waited for quite some time before Manjit Kaur appeared.

During the interval they did not speak at all, but sat quietly, waiting. The impression Hetty had taken away with her after their first meeting with Manjit Kaur was of a very ordinary English sitting-room. This time she observed differences that pointed to another culture — though separately these items seen elsewhere would have meant nothing other than exotic taste. Here the few Indian silk cushions, a low table that was heavily carved, the spicy fragrance of an Indian incense, indicated something more, maybe the desire not to lose the familiar traditions of home.

On several occasions they could hear the sound of a raised, male voice. Hetty did not think it was Sobha because the timbre was lower, more forceful. She wondered how long it would be before they were shown the door. Eventually Manjit Kaur and Jit came in together.

Hetty stood up. 'It is very good of you to receive us, Mrs Singh. Megan has something she wants to tell you.'

'I do not believe that Megan has anything to say that will be of any interest to me,' said Mrs Singh inexorably, 'now or in the future.'

'Ma,' protested Jit.

'You see, we all believed that Megan was Jit's friend,' Mrs Singh continued, as though her daughter had not spoken. 'We could not have known that she would betray that friendship in the way she has done. We, that is, Jit's father and I, think there is no point in this interview. I suggest you both leave at once.'

'Mrs Singh, if that is your wish, then of course we must go, but, please, will you listen for just five minutes?' said Hetty desperately, for Megan was looking absolutely stricken. 'There are certain matters that I am sure Megan can clear up to your satisfaction, if you would hear us out.'

'As if anyone could get any satisfaction out of the shame of a niece!'

'There is no shame. Mrs Singh . . . Megan . . . '

'Mrs Singh, Balbiro said she wanted to leave her family for a few days to think about her marriage quietly. I invited her to come and stay with me.'

'In your father's house,' Manjit Kaur interrupted harshly. 'And you have no mother. You were living there alone at the time.'

'I was alone for all but twenty-four hours of that time.'

'Mrs Singh, Balbiro was perfectly safe. No harm came to her at all. Both girls are over eighteen. There was nothing wrong in them being without a parent.'

'Until the brother arrived. Oh, yes. We know about the brother. Balbiro confessed.'

'There was nothing to confess to,' Megan broke in. 'Jake came to see me because we haven't seen each other since Christmas. He stayed for one night before driving to Heathrow for his flight.'

'He stayed one night.'

'Miss Loveridge, this is awful,' said Megan, her breathing fast and shallow. 'I have to get my father. He's in the car. Perhaps he could speak to Mr Singh?'

'I don't think . . . '

'Maybe if the men were to talk together we might continue this on our own?' suggested Hetty. 'We are here to ask you to let us help Balbiro and her family. We do not want to make more trouble.'

Manjit Kaur nodded her head slowly. 'Jit, go with Megan.' She sat down. 'It is good of you to come to the assistance of your students,' she said to Hetty, 'when this is none of your business.'

'I know it is not a problem of mine,' Hetty said calmly, ignoring the barbed comment, 'but you were kind enough to ask me to Jit's wedding and so I do feel very much involved. Forgive me, but were there repercussions for Jit? I see that her husband is with you.'

Manjit Kaur grimaced. 'For a time I was convinced that Balbiro's shame was going to affect Jit. I think that if we had still been in Punjab he would have cast her off. Then I think he remembered in time all the trouble we had gone to in order to procure him a visa and a home and a job in this country. I expect you think me disloyal to my family to speak this way about my son-in-law? He is a good

145

boy,' she insisted. 'He will be kind to Jit. I tell you this because we are women together and there are times when the values — no, not the values — the . . . ' she shrugged. 'I cannot explain.'

'The sensibilities of women,' Hetty offered. 'Our common sense,' she explained as Manjit Kaur seemed not to understand. 'I'm sorry, I was thinking of Jane Austen.'

'Ah, *Bride and Prejudice*,' said Manjit Kaur brightly. 'I enjoyed that film. I love all the Bollywood movies. They remind me of home. There are times when I long for home. And,' she added sombrely, 'had we been in Punjab none of this would have happened.'

'Is Jit truly happy with her marriage?' Hetty asked boldly.

'You do not have the right to ask that.'

'Maybe not, but I ask it all the same. You must know that the school went to a lot of trouble to make sure that Jit had a good offer for a place at Cardiff. It is something we do for all our students. No one at the school ever expected her to abandon everything for an arranged marriage.'

'You speak bluntly.'

'I am outraged by what seems to me to be the waste of a girl's life. You will forgive me for speaking candidly but further education is something we, in this country, expect for all

146

of our young women if they have the ability to profit by it. Further education is the means by which a young woman is able to find a good job. In the end this benefits not only her but her family.'

Manjit Kaur bit her lip. 'I see you do feel strongly about this.'

'You could not expect otherwise, from a woman who teaches and is unmarried,' Hetty persisted. 'Mrs Singh, I believe I recall Jit telling me that you yourself are a qualified doctor.'

'That is so.' Mrs Singh bowed her head regally. 'But I gave up my work once I was married.'

'And your daughter is expected to abandon her hopes of becoming a teacher, any idea of qualifications, because of her marriage at eighteen?'

There was a small pause.

'Her father and I . . . No one has explained these matters to my son-in-law. It is the way we do things at home.'

'I think you will find that Jit considers this to be her home.' Again Hetty decided to be blunt.

'It is possible that Sobha might agree that Jit should continue her education while he learns English and the way we do things here,' Mrs Singh said quietly.

As a concession it was a start, thought Hetty. But there was no time to force a promise for Mr Singh entered the room accompanied by both Tom Gillard and Sobha Singh.

★ ★ ★

Lingering behind the men, Jit grasped Megan by the arm and dragged her into the kitchen. There, she closed the door quietly and turned to face her friend.

'It was never meant to end this way, was it?' she cried softly.

'Of course it wasn't,' said Megan. 'I guess you all think it's my fault? I suppose it is my fault. I told you when we were waiting for the bus that I did what I thought was the right thing. I mean, how could I have just handed over £100 and left Balbiro to go to Birmingham on her own? She told me she had a map and knew exactly where to find the woman's refuge, but I just couldn't, Jit. That's why I persuaded her to come to stay.'

'If only your brother hadn't arrived. That's what's bad, innit?'

'That's what they are all saying. But he was great. I mean, Jake was really good with Balbiro. He said that the best thing would be for her to speak to Resham, text him, anything. If they could just communicate.'

'Why do you think she gave in?'

'I think as time went by she got scared. I know I'd be scared.'

'There's another thing — '

'Jit, I'm so sorry,' Megan interrupted impulsively.

The girls looked at each other soberly for a moment. Then they hugged each other. 'Has it — has it made a difference with you and Sobha?' Megan asked diffidently.

Jit put her head on one side. Then she smiled. It was a smile full of meaning. 'It shook him. I think he hadn't realized that British Sikhs are different from the ones at home. He doesn't seem to mind, though.'

At that moment the kitchen door opened and Sobha Singh entered. 'Your ma,' he said. 'She say come.'

'We'd better go,' said Jit. She squeezed her friend's hand. 'See you, Megan.'

★ ★ ★

'Mr Gillard has assured me that his son has a most excellent reputation. Balbiro would not have been left alone with him for any time at all,' Balbir Singh was telling his wife. 'So it would appear that maybe we have been a little hasty.' It was an admission that emerged with reluctance, as though the man did not care for it to be assumed that he could have jumped to a conclusion that was blatantly unjust.

'What I cannot understand is how anyone came to know about Jake's presence,' said Tom. 'Megan tells me that she and Balbiro never left the house until Balbiro decided she would go home. There cannot be any disgrace attached to either of them.'

'Not to your daughter, I agree. But matters are different with us. That Balbiro should leave her parents' home, without their permission, to go to stay with a stranger for several days, is disgraceful. Of course she was punished.'

Hetty winced at his words, thinking that she knew what form this punishment had taken. She hoped the beating had not been too bad.

'Mr Singh, I understand that Balbiro knew the young man, Resham, when they were young children. That would imply he is well acquainted with our ways, as would Resham's parents be also.'

'I do not see your point, Miss Loveridge.'

'I am surprised they were not permitted time alone together. Not in this day and age. If they had spoken alone or had been encouraged to show their feelings maybe this

150

would never have happened.'

'It was Resham himself who wanted to uphold our traditions.'

'So noble, so misguided,' sighed Hetty.

There was an awkward pause as Hetty sat staring into space and Balbir Singh frowned mightily.

'Who, precisely, is accusing Balbiro of committing anything more than a small indiscretion? Is it her husband? If so, he should have had the courtesy of coming to speak to me, Megan and Jake's father,' Tom intervened.

For a moment Mr Singh appeared nonplussed. 'Actually, Resham has not repudiated Balbiro. Not yet. I understand he is quite prepared to accept her as his wife since he has loved her for many years.'

'Then I do not understand,' said Tom in his turn.

'The family had explained Balbiro's absence by saying that she was staying with an aunt. Balbiro's brother, Keval, wrung a confession from her, that she had run away, that she had been in a young man's company while she was away. He could not keep that a secret.'

'I trust Keval did not tell the whole world this distorted version of the truth,' said Tom drily.

'There is more. You see, since Balbiro left the *Gurdwara* with Keval, she has not been seen.'

'Where is she?' asked Hetty.

'We do not know,' said Manjit Kaur heavily. 'She has disappeared and no one can find her.'

# 8

They had not stayed longer in Chepstow. Mrs Singh made to offer them some refreshments but Tom looked at Hetty, who read correctly in his eyes that he would prefer to be anywhere else than where he was. With that she concurred fervently and the journey home was punctuated by Megan's exclamations of horror, astonishment and speculation, the chief one being:

'What do you think they are really doing to find Balbiro?'

It was the question Megan had asked Mrs Singh. The reply had been evasive but at the time no one had felt they had the right to persist.

Hetty said now, 'They must have gone to the police.'

'There is no must about it,' said Tom. 'Balbiro is over eighteen. In this country she has the perfect right to leave home without telling anyone.'

'She can't just disappear. Not after what happened,' insisted Megan. 'It has been made to seem a scandal. Someone has to put that right. The Singhs even admitted to us that

Balbiro had been forced to confess about Jake. If that doesn't sound sinister, I'd like to know what does.'

'Don't be dramatic,' said her father wearily.

'It is worrying, though.' Privately Hetty was inclined to agree with Megan though she thought it wiser to keep that to herself for the moment.

'She'll turn up,' said Tom confidently, 'in a few days.'

'Will you let me know if you hear anything more about Balbiro?' Hetty asked as she got into her car, which she had left at the cottage. She had declined Tom's pressing invitation to stay for supper, feeling that because so much had happened since she had arrived for tea, she was very much in need of the peace and quiet of her own home.

'I don't know that I will hear anything more for a few weeks,' said Megan, a cloud crossing her face. 'I won't be here. That's why I'm so worried about what Balbiro's family is doing about finding her.'

'Megan is going to stay with my sister and her family. She spends a month with them every summer, though usually earlier than this.'

Neither Tom nor Megan had thought to mention to Hetty before that this was an arrangement that had been in place since

Megan's mother had died. Tom's sister, Gillian, and her husband, Stephen, invited Megan to stay at their home then took her away with their own two children on their family holiday. It had been a godsend for Tom, whose summer had been made so much easier without the pressing need to look after a child on his own during the whole of the long school holidays. This year the Giles family was to go to France.

'They're taking a gîte in Normandy. Uncle Stephen wants to see the Bayeux Tapestry,' said Megan. 'We're staying in a sort of modern complex and there's a swimming pool so I suppose it won't be too much of a bore.'

'How banal. The Bayeux Tapestry is magnificent,' said Tom.

'Your father is absolutely right,' declared Hetty.

'I guess this will be the last time we're all together, too. Pete is my age and he's been complaining about going on family holidays for a couple of years now. Once he starts at Exeter he won't want to know us,' said Megan, with a sigh. It was with Peter she had first experimented with sex — a short-lived event which had been transformed into a firm friendship by the following summer, both preferring to forget adolescent fumblings as if they had never happened.

'I expect you'll be company for Kate for a time, though.'

'Kate is fourteen.'

A bit young, thought Hetty. She wondered how Tom and Gillian would react when Megan herself decided she wanted something a little more challenging for her summer vacation. 'So you won't be back for a month?'

'That's right. Then I'm going to be busy getting ready for uni so that's the rest of the summer taken care of.'

'Oh.' Hetty absorbed the news while she fastened her seat belt, aware that Megan sounded both excited and unenthusiastic at the same time. 'Is that why you are so bothered about Balbiro? You know, I really don't think we can do anything more than we already have.'

'Of course we can't,' said Tom bracingly. 'It is their concern, not ours. Balbiro's family, I mean.'

'If I had more time I could go looking for her,' suggested Megan.

'Not a good idea,' said Hetty quickly, before Tom could protest. 'You would have no notion where to start.' The thought of the quite appalling places Megan might think fit to search sent shivers down her spine. 'Once the family has been able to convince the police she is a missing person, they are the best people to do that sort of thing.'

'If they do go to the police.'

'Leave it, Meg,' said Tom sharply. 'And that is not a request.'

'It has to be left to the family for a few more days before anyone can think of interfering, and then you won't be here,' said Hetty. 'Look, if it would set your mind at rest, why don't I keep in touch with Jit and if I hear anything I'll let you know. Perhaps you could give me an address?'

'I don't suppose Megan has her address in France,' said Tom quickly. 'Much better let me know and I'll pass it on.'

Megan's eyes narrowed. 'Much better, Miss Loveridge,' she agreed woodenly.

Hetty glanced at her suspiciously. 'Fine,' she said, closed the door and started the engine. 'See you, Tom,' she said through the wound-down window.

'Er, yes. When?'

'On Saturday, I suppose. At the garden.'

'You won't . . . No. Fine. Saturday . . . ' But the car was already halfway down the potholed lane.

'Dad, you are an idiot,' said Megan fondly. 'Poor Hetty wasn't ever going to prolong this. Not after that encounter with the Singhs. She looks exhausted. Besides, you've got her telephone number. You know where she lives.'

'I don't know what on earth you mean,' said her father loftily.

★ ★ ★

Hetty needed to go shopping the following morning. She made sure the answer phone was on — and somehow never got to turn it off when she came home. However, the decision as to whether to answer a call, or call back, did not have to be made, either that day or the next. She duly kept her appointment with her solicitor in Monmouth and was relieved to hear that since nothing untoward had emerged it looked as though probate on her mother's estate would be granted with the minimum of delay.

'Not that I expect to do anything extravagant, now or in the future,' Hetty said firmly, when her solicitor asked if she intended treating herself. Polly Firmer, younger than Hetty, was newly arrived in her practice in Monmouth.

'Of course not. Time is at a premium when you are working,' agreed Polly, 'but you will be able to afford the odd exotic holiday in the summer now. That could be fun.'

Hetty could see in her face that Polly meant she could meet men, enlarge her social

158

circle, make something of herself. She prevented her lip curling with difficulty. 'Or I could save it for a long cruise when I've retired,' she said, her face still expressionless.

Polly opened her mouth, then closed it. 'Sorry,' she said. 'I never meant to imply . . . '

'Of course you didn't,' said Hetty, relenting. 'I just meant that I don't expect my life will change a great deal.'

'It is more than a comfortable sum your mother left.'

'When I thought I was lucky to be just comfortable.'

'So one thing you really should be thinking about is making your own will,' Polly persisted. 'Everyone should do that, whatever their estate.'

'I know. I'll make an appointment for next week and think about it in the meantime.'

Oh dear, Hetty reflected as she left the office. Apart from a goddaughter who had recently married and gone abroad, who was there to whom she might leave her worldly goods? It was a sobering moment. Fifty-two next birthday and quite without anyone of significance in her life.

But I'm damned if it'll go to a cats' home, she thought.

At breakfast on Thursday the phone rang. Hetty picked it up without thinking. But the caller was not Tom Gillard.

'Hetty? It's Clive. Clive Makepeace.'

'Hello, Clive. This is unexpected. I do hope you weren't going to ask me to work today because I'm very busy,' said Hetty firmly, determined not to become a pushover as far as The Grange was concerned. 'But Saturday is fine,' she added hastily, because neither did she want to sound churlish.

'I just wondered if you were free tonight.'

'Free . . . '

'You see, I heard that you are interested in seeing the inside of the castle and I happened to mention it to Mary Beresford yesterday and she wondered if you would like to come and have a drink with them this evening then have a private guided tour.' It emerged in a rush, almost as though he had been practising.

'Oh,' said Hetty. 'Well, that's very kind of her but . . . '

'Mary would have phoned you herself but I didn't have your number on me. I have to talk to Ian about something financial, so she suggested I picked you up and we came over together. What do you say?'

'Well . . . Fine,' said Hetty, trying to inject some eagerness into her voice. 'I'd enjoy that.'

They settled on six o'clock and she

replaced the receiver, not sure quite what to think. She did, indeed, want to see over the castle, but she had certainly not expected the invitation to be issued so soon, nor by Clive Makepeace. She did hope she was not being foisted on the Beresfords by him.

Hetty decided on navy linen trousers, a cream short-sleeved top and a yellow jacket. Boring, she thought, and added a necklace of yellow glass flowers she had bought only the previous morning in Vera's gallery — a sop to Polly's insistence that she should treat herself? Smart enough for a drink, practical (her shoes were flat), but definitely not in the expected guest category.

Did she see disappointment in Clive Makepeace's face? All to the good, Hetty decided. Her reward was Mary Beresford's approval when they met in the kitchen, a huge room that seemed to do duty as living-room and office as well as its proper purpose, for Ian was chopping vegetables.

'Hi,' said Mary. 'Have a glass of wine. White?' Mary, sitting at an old oak desk surrounded by papers when they arrived, was jeans-clad, and she was wearing trainers that had seen better days.

'What Mary means is we've run out of red.' Ian Beresford's shirt was frayed at both collar and cuffs (though Clive was natty in a clean

161

shirt, seersucker jacket and heavily pressed linen trousers).

'White is excellent. Thanks,' said Hetty, accepting the glass. 'I know Clive wants to talk to Ian so I do hope I'm not an imposition.'

'I've been aching for an excuse to leave these for ages.'

Beyond the kitchen there was the sound of a door slamming, the blare of a raucous children's TV show and discordant recorder practice.

'Turn that television off, Jack, and shut the door quietly whoever slammed it!' yelled Ian. 'Mary, does Emma really need to practise in the same room as her brother?'

'Of course not. I'll sort it.'

Family matters attended to, Mary came back to where Hetty was examining an old, framed plan of the estate. 'Drink up, then we'll leave the men to it while I show you round.'

The Beresfords were a couple in their late thirties. Rumour had it that Ian had made a killing on the stock exchange when he was still under twenty-five — though as he was a private man there were only a very few friends who could attest to the truth of this and none of them would have been so indiscreet. Ian had bought Ottergate some twelve years previously and he and Mary had devoted themselves to the castle and its grounds ever since while at the same time bringing up their two children, Jack, aged twelve, and Emma, now ten.

Ottergate, one of the line of defensive castles built by the order of William the Conqueror in the Marches to contain the Welsh, sat strategically at the head of a long, narrow valley at the end of which was Otterhaven. As castles go, it had never been particularly commanding, neither had it been the site of any major battle nor even a minor skirmish. Even Cromwell's soldiers appear to have been unaware of its existence, so it remained as it had always been, more of a fortified family home. But Ottergate had been in the ownership of no less than six families over the years, whose wealth and power declined each time the castle changed hands, and inevitably it had suffered from neglect.

Constructed just below the brow of a hill from which it was afforded long views without suffering too much from the prevailing winds, Ottergate was today roughly half its former size, the main two-storeyed L-shaped house being the remnant of the great hall, the kitchens and the original motte. A high stone wall was also attached to the house, and against this stood a few useful lean-to outbuildings, probably late Georgian, forming two sides of the cobbled courtyard. The remaining side — in which was the solid wooden gate through which Clive and Hetty had entered — was now an indeterminate ruin.

'We understand that the configurations of the castle conform more or less to the original plan,' said Mary Beresford, 'though logically they must have changed over the centuries, but obviously whatever changes were made, the original stone was re-used. What has been lost is the gate-house, two small towers there and there' — she indicated their sites — 'and the fortified wall connecting them. There are remains of what must have been an outer bailey where the walled garden is. Ian thinks the walls of that were made from its old stone.'

'It must have been quite a sight in its heyday,' commented Hetty.

'We're not even sure when that was, exactly. Personally I'm very happy with what we have. At least that's just about manage-able. Come and see the rest of the house.'

'It's very good of you to show me round.' Hetty hesitated. 'It must be a bore to show people round your home.'

'Not at all. It's satisfying to be able to demonstrate that something with as long a history as this has still makes a fantastic family home. I should explain,' she said, her attitude an endearing mixture of determination and uncertainty, and stopped.

'Go on,' encouraged Hetty, intrigued.

'You see, Ian's nephew had a leukaemia when he was only five. He's cured now, we hope and pray, but it needed a bone marrow transplant and none of us, none of his family, was compatible. Oliver was one of the lucky ones whose donor came from the national register. You can't imagine how shattering it is to have a child whose life depends on the generosity of a total stranger,' she ended abruptly, tears in her eyes, which she rubbed away fiercely.

'How dreadful,' murmured Hetty inadequately, who had known of other families in similar situations because of the nature of her work but who understood that she would never experience the helplessness they felt.

'So,' said Mary brightly, 'I am now an active supporter of a leukaemia charity. I fundraise. Ian and I both know we have to recoup some of our outlay on the castle. We also agree that we have to balance our desire for privacy with the obvious way of making money by opening to the public on set days, but that is what we plan to do. It's useful to show someone round who is really interested in order to get feedback. The Grange already has regular open days which I hope Clive has told you about.'

'He's not told me anything. You see,' said Hetty, determined to set the record straight, 'I've only met Clive once before and that was when I first came to the garden to work.'

Mary Beresford laughed. It was a friendly laugh and there was a definite twinkle in her eye as she replied, 'Do you know, I had a feeling it was something like that.'

'Excuse me? I think I've lost you. I don't know anything about him, you see, except that he's a keen gardener. That's why I was a little concerned about — '

'Meeting us? I'm very glad he brought you over. As I said, it's great to meet someone who has a feel for places like this.'

Hetty glowed. 'I'm not knowledgeable, but I do appreciate anything with a sense of history.'

'I knew it. Mind you, there's quite a history behind Clive.'

'Oh, yes?'

'I'm not really being indiscreet, or relaying gossip, but you might want to know that Clive, who is a dear man, lost his wife a couple of years ago. Apparently she had been an invalid for many years. Poor Clive had been forced to take early retirement to nurse

166

her and once she died he decided to pull up his roots — which were in Somerset — and start afresh. You're right about his horticultural knowledge. He was the manager of a large garden centre and so what he doesn't know about coping with this place isn't worth worrying about. We are so lucky that he is as keen on us as we are on him. The thing is . . . ' For the first time Mary seemed a little uncomfortable. 'Clive has obviously got over the loss of his wife. He — he seems to hanker after female companionship. I just thought you might want to know.'

'Ah,' said Hetty wisely. 'It's not just me; it's the fact that I wear a skirt.'

They both looked at Hetty's trousers and giggled girlishly.

'Exactly so. You see that we've been able to convert part of the L into a four-bedroomed dwelling that is reasonably modern.' Mary, who had led Hetty into the house once more, reverted to the subject which was undoubtedly more dear to her. 'We are now just coming to the end of restoring the rest back into what it might have looked before the twentieth century. No electricity, therefore no electric light, no central heating. I plan to have medieval banquets — not the rowdy sort, I hasten to add — using authentic recipes, home-grown food flavoured with our

167

own herbs and so on and musical entertainment using authentic instruments.'

'Goodness,' said Hetty faintly.

'For The Grange's open days I dry our flowers and sell them, make lavender bags and potpourri. I make jam from our soft fruit. Then we keep bees and I sell the honey, and next year I have promised myself that I shall have candles and soap to add to our stock.'

'Goodness,' Hetty repeated. 'However do you have the time?'

'By shamelessly using voluntary labour in The Grange — which the girls are happy to give because it's for charity — and naturally by accepting any offers anyone likes to make,' Mary said candidly, referring affectionately to their elderly volunteers.

'I have a full-time job.'

'I know. Clive said. I just thought I'd mention it.'

'On the other hand I would be very interested to learn more about the old processes and now that I am on my own I don't see why I can't spare the odd few hours occasionally.'

'That's fantastic. Lots of what I do is seasonal and it's difficult to find people who have that sort of time to spare.' She added, 'Clive told me about your mother's death. That must have been a shock for you.'

'It was,' admitted Hetty, her voice a little choked. 'I — we'd no idea she even had a problem. When someone dies suddenly you feel cheated; guilty that things were left unsaid.'

'And there's the empty house.'

'That's just it. You sound as though you've been through it yourself.'

'Not in quite the same way. But my mother also died suddenly and it appears that my father couldn't live without her, even though he was perfectly robust and under seventy. He survived her by only six months. I remember he said that the very worst thing was the empty house which nevertheless echoed with the sound of her voice. You don't have children, do you?'

'I've never married.'

Mary smiled gently. 'Not the same thing today, is it? Did you never want children? Ah. You must forgive me. I have this dreadful habit of asking impertinent questions. Ian is always warning me about it.'

'Working in a girls' school isn't conducive to marriage. No, that's not strictly true. There were . . . I have . . . Well, no need to go into that. You see, I never felt the need to go looking for a man — the special man. And as for children, though I've always enjoyed the teaching, encouraging young minds to

169

stretch, seeing them mature, I've always been relieved in a quiet sort of way to close the door behind the bustle of school and the children. Does that make me seem one-dimensional, selfish?'

'Not at all. I imagine that if you are a really good teacher you must be giving so much of yourself daily that you need to recoup your energies in peace and quiet.'

'As I say, it's the way I am and now it appears I'm stuck with it. Though now I come to think of it there could come a time when I miss having grandchildren. They must be a joy.'

'Clive has a married son who lives in London,' observed Mary. 'I'm not sure about grandchildren.'

'There are former pupils with whom I have a continuing good relationship, so I can't be entirely a lost cause,' said Hetty defensively, wondering whether to mention Megan as an example. Then innate caution warned her that in talking about Megan she would have to mention the girl's father. Mary must know Tom Gillard. And no one would be expected to forget to mention Tom Gillard. Mary might only have been frank about Clive Makepeace because she was anxious to be friendly; she might not be quite so circum-spect about Tom.

They returned to the kitchen, where it appeared the men had finished their business.

'I'd like to ask you both to stay for something to eat,' said Mary apologetically, 'but there's no way two pork chops will stretch to four.'

'Of course not,' said Hetty, reaching for her bag, which she'd left on an old settle. 'We must get going, mustn't we, Clive?' she ended firmly, seeing hesitation in the man's face. 'Thanks so much for the drink, Ian, and the tour, Mary, and why don't I give you a ring in a day or so and perhaps you could let me know the next project that wants another pair of hands?'

'That would be great. Hetty, I'll keep you to that.'

'Don't tell me,' groaned Ian. 'She's done the spiel again and played on the sympathy strings?'

'I'm hooked,' admitted Hetty cheerfully. 'So maybe I'll see you both soon. Bye.'

'Pity about the chops,' said Clive wistfully, as he opened the car door for Hetty. 'Ian is a fantastic cook.'

'I wasn't expecting to be asked to stay for a meal,' replied Hetty. 'I mean, not after the first meeting. We mightn't have got on at all.'

'Which I see is far from the truth.'

Did he sound censorious or was it perhaps

a touch of jealousy? 'Clive, I do like the sound of Mary's plans but I wouldn't dream of going back on my promise to help with the garden,' she said gently.

'That's all right, then.'

Hetty sighed inwardly. Whatever the truth about Clive's needing female companionship, there was plainly going to be little encouragement from him tonight, even dressed up as they were. 'I could do with something to eat, though,' she said. 'But I'm afraid that I only planned on bread and cheese tonight so why don't I buy us something at a pub to say thank you for organizing a very intriguing evening.'

'Oh, I say. Well,' he said, brightening visibly, 'that's a good idea. I hear The Duck and Drake does good pub food and it's only a mile or so out of our way. Of course I couldn't let you pay.'

'My idea,' insisted Hetty, 'or I go straight home.'

'I guess there'll be other occasions,' he gave in. 'I do like a woman who knows her own mind.'

'The Duck and Drake it is, then' Hetty groaned inwardly, wondering what she had just set in motion with Clive and hoping fervently that she would not live to regret her overture.

Balbiro's Journal, 23rd July

Of course I capitulated after the beating.

Not immediately. I became feverish so I wasn't able to talk much for a few days. My mother was furious with my father and threatened to send for a doctor. He told her that she knew enough about fevers to be able to cope on her own.

She was kind to me.

She was much kinder than my brother. Though Keval didn't touch me. He just kept on and on.

Who had I seen?

Did I really expect them to believe that I had seen only my school-friend, Megan, while I was away from home?

How had Megan and I got to Chepstow? Did Megan really have a car of her own?

I can't remember how I slipped up but in the end they discovered about Jake. I mean, what was there to discover?

Keval is becoming so fanatical. Years ago he had plenty of English friends himself. Girls he met in nightclubs. There was even a special one. He was seen with her several times. Mandy, I think her name was. I remember teasing him about her and he wasn't offended. I don't know anything more about her and I certainly never met her. He was a bit scathing about her actually, calling her all sorts of names. I was shocked, though I never thought it would amount to anything. I knew that Keval would only consider marrying a Sikh girl whom his family had found for him.

So, yes, I confessed that Megan's brother was at the cottage.

You'd have thought the heavens had opened.

At least they didn't beat me again.

It was my mother who insisted that we must keep the whole thing a secret, that if we didn't speak about it no one would ever know. It is not often that Ma has that steely note in her voice. But both Keval and my father saw sense very quickly. Ma had already told a neighbour, Mrs Cooper who lived next door and who was being inquisitive, that I had gone to Chepstow to visit my aunt. Once I was seen by Mrs Cooper again no one would say anything more.

As soon as I could stand up straight they made me dress and accompany my mother to the shops. It wasn't nice but I could understand that it was necessary. We saw several neighbours and I told them that I'd had a pleasant stay with my Aunty Manjit and my cousin, Jit, in Chepstow.

'That's your cousin who is marrying at the same time, isn't it?'

'That's right,' Ma answered. 'Such a wedding it is going to be.'

'Are you getting excited about your wedding?' Mrs Cooper asked.

'Oh, yes,' I said.

Everyone seemed satisfied.

# 9

Perusing the menu at The Duck and Drake, Hetty settled for the sea bass and agreed that a bottle of Oyster Bay Sauvignon Blanc would go well with both that and Clive's salmon. The pub was one she did not know — not that Hetty's knowledge of pubs in general could be said to be in-depth. She was pleased to discover that this one had not been altered substantially so that it appeared to have a genuine atmosphere.

While they were waiting to be served, they talked desultorily about the convenience of where she lived in the centre of Otterhaven as opposed to his own house, which was in a newly built development on the edge of the village. 'Veronica hated old houses. She said they were too expensive to maintain and too difficult to keep clean. Maybe that's why I bought a new one again. Mind you,' he added darkly, 'I've already found that modern builders can be extremely slapdash. You wouldn't want to know what I've had to put right.'

'Probably not,' agreed Hetty, then saw she had offended him and said quickly, 'it must have been a bore for you.'

'But the worst thing about it is that it is too far to walk carrying the shopping. I hate having to take the car out every time I leave the house.'

'Walking can take time but it is good for you,' said Hetty, smug in the ownership of a bicycle to which she had already admitted. 'I suppose it must have seemed a good idea to you when you moved here.'

'The last thing I wanted at the time was to have to cope with renovations so I settled for something that would be easily saleable in the future, if ever I wanted to move again.'

Their food arrived and both agreed that they had made good choices.

'An easily saleable house was a very sensible buy,' Hetty commented. 'Mary told me that you'd been widowed just before you came to Otterhaven. You must have had a sad time of it.'

'Even though it was by no means unexpected, losing Veronica was most unsettling.'

'It's a strange way of putting it, but I do know what you mean. I still can't get over the fact that I'll never again find my mother inside the cottage waiting for me after school. Apart from my university years, she was always there. I even commuted for two years to my first teaching post in Bristol.'

'So that means you went to school in Otterhaven?'

'Doesn't that make me sound parochial? Yes, I'm teaching at my old school. Not a speck of adventure in my genes, I'm afraid.'

'I think continuity is a splendid thing. It isn't given to many of us.'

'Mary said you have a son?'

'James. He's a research chemist and lives in Reading.'

'Do you get to see him often? At least Reading's the right side of London for a quick visit.'

'James found his mother somewhat difficult, unsympathetic. They had a thorny relationship which never seemed to improve over the years and he only visited when duty called, like Christmas.' Clive grimaced. 'There wasn't much I could do to change that, even when she was very ill, especially as James's wife supported him. I had thought that marriage and fatherhood would alter his attitude, but it hasn't worked out quite as I hoped it would.'

'That's sad. Do you have grandchildren?'

'A grandson of eight, called Mark. Lindy, who is a midwife, insists that she will only have the one child.'

'One day Mark'll be old enough to stay

177

with you on his own. You'll have to work on that. After all, now that you are free to go where you want, you can always visit them. It must have been extremely delicate trying to maintain the relationship when Veronica was ill.'

'And it has to be said that I failed. Feeling able to visit them is a good idea, in theory. Unfortunately, very often things don't work out as we wish. Then there's The Grange. That takes up a lot of my time.'

The waiter removed their plates. Hetty was thinking that Clive could do something about his situation if he truly desired it — that maybe the exertion required seemed too daunting. She thought then, complacently, how fortunate she was to have avoided the snags of family relationships, which were full of baggage. How so much simpler was her own life. But was it going to be dreadfully dull in the future? Now that was a novel concept.

'There is always the possibility of change,' she said brightly. She saw that Clive was inclined to refute this, as she had expected so, adopting the tactics used by Mary earlier on herself, she continued, 'Tell me how you came to be involved with The Grange. It's quite something to have agreed to do.'

'Were you going to add 'at my age'?'

'Not at all.'

'I'm sixty-one.'

'And young-looking at that,' she grinned. She thought, aghast, I think I'm flirting. What is it with me nowadays?

Clive flushed, though whether in appreciation of the flattery or because he was aware of the momentary frisson his expression did not reveal. 'I met Ian at an antiquarians' meeting soon after I arrived in Otterhaven. He suggested I might like to have a look at Ottergate's garden. At the time the Beresfords hadn't decided just what to do with it, though Ian did say that restoring the garden formed part of their longterm plans. It was in a dreadful mess — obviously hadn't been touched for years.'

How animated a man became when he was passionate about an interest, Hetty was thinking as she listened to Clive describing the state of the garden when he first saw it: derelict, over-run with brambles and nettles and self-sown saplings, its walls breached in places.

'But the interesting thing was that the basic structure was still there, beneath all the undergrowth. The lines of the paths and the beds were as they must have been years ago. The fruit trees are old species — such fantastic luck — and nothing has been sprayed for two generations, which will give us accreditation with the Soil Association. Even some of the ancient box hedging was there, though it was too far gone to save. Ian asked me to draw up a scheme of work — for a fee, I might add, as he's a very fair man to work for. And when I'd done that — bearing in mind the cost and the time involved — we agreed that I'd be retained for a few hours every week to get the garden started.'

'I bet you put in more hours than in the original agreement,' Hetty said.

'I suppose I do. You see, Hetty, this whole thing is so amazingly grandiose in its conception, when you think about it. Regenerating a walled garden is totally satisfying. I expect you know that walled gardens began as pleasure gardens. Later their purpose was to feed the household. Nowadays we are beginning to think of them in terms of pleasure again, certainly the smaller ones. Of course it's been done before — Aberglasney near Llandeilo is a good Welsh example — but I never thought I'd have the opportunity to become involved in anything like that, though The Grange is very much less exalted than Aberglasney.'

'So you are going to make The Grange into a pleasure garden?'

'Not entirely. Mary wants us to grow some

fruit, vegetables and flowers for her to use in the castle. The idea is that we transfer the vegetables she has planted near the kitchen into the walled garden, add flowers for cutting and preserving and make the flowerbeds near the castle itself simply decorative. And now Ian has agreed the funds for a knot garden for herbs.'

'It sounds exciting, but a great deal of work.'

'Which is where the volunteers come in — and, as you mentioned, my added hours. You see, the money I'm paid doesn't matter — my pension is secure, fortunately, and I have enough for my needs — and to be a part of this is literally awe-inspiring.'

'You're a lucky man,' Hetty observed. She had declined the coffee Clive wanted and was toying with a final glass of wine.

'Lucky? I must say I'd never considered myself to be a particularly fortunate man.'

'I know you've lost your wife, but to have a totally satisfying profession which will occupy you for as long as you wish it to, friends . . . '

'I don't have too many of those.'

'I understood otherwise.'

'From Mary? I hope you didn't listen to too much gossip.'

'I don't believe Mary gossips,' said Hetty quietly. 'All she told me was that you are a

181

widower.' She permitted herself the little white lie. After all, to her mind LWLs oiled the wheels of social intercourse. There was absolutely no need to let Clive know that it was generally recognized he was actively seeking female companionship, was there? 'I think it's time we went,' she said, and signalled to the waiter for the bill.

'Are you sure you . . . Of course. We must do this again,' he said.

'That would be nice, but I warn you, I'm getting behind in my preparation for next year. If you want me to be free on Saturdays you must remember that. And please don't give me the teachers-have-such-long-holidays guff. You really would be surprised how much work we have to get through in our so-called holidays.'

'You make me weep,' said Clive, smiling with his first attempt at genuine humour Hetty had heard. 'I'll ring you.'

'After Saturday.'

★   ★   ★

Otterhaven boasted two small dress shops. One catered strictly for the under twenty-fives, trendy denim, the current miniscule chemise tops and several displays of cheap and fashionable jewellery. From the outside the other resembled nothing more than a charity shop, with its racks of tightly packed items — though there was no attempt to segregate trousers from tops or frocks. Charity shop it was not: Dolly's prices were anything but cheap. If you had the strength, and the time, (preferably both), you went in and searched for what you were looking for in your size and colour and took it to a cubicle (fortunately the open changing-room had never hit Dolly's). Seeing there was a sale advertised in the window, on impulse Hetty decided she could do with a frock and entered to join five others jostling for the early bargains.

One of these bargain hunters was Mary Beresford.

'Caught in the act,' said Mary. 'Don't tell Ian but we are going to a garden party next week and I haven't a thing to wear.'

'I promise I won't breathe a word.'

'I've found this,' said Mary doubtfully, 'but it isn't really my colour.' It was a floaty frock in a brilliant yellow print. 'Bit too mother-of-the-bride, I think.'

'It does depend what else you might want it for.'

'Precisely. I might add it to the pile, though. There is something you might like.' Mary, noticing that Hetty was also looking at frocks, hauled it out, a wisteria-blue silk splashed with large white flowers.

Hetty, who had draped a short-sleeved navy spotted linen over her arm, looked askance, both at the dress and the price. 'Well . . . '

'Try it.'

They spent a happy half-hour trying on several items apiece. In the end Mary took the yellow frock and Hetty bought both the navy spotted linen (sensible but with a dash of élan) and the wisteria-blue (which was romantic and did something extraordinary to her eyes).

'Did you enjoy last evening?'

'It was so good of you to show me round the castle. Thank you, again.'

'You know I didn't mean that. Your dinner with Clive.'

'What makes you think I didn't go straight home?'

'As if.'

'As a matter of fact we did have something to eat.'

'Anywhere nice?'

'The Duck and Drake.'

'Good choice. I hope you didn't go Dutch.'

'It was at my invitation.'

'Oh, well. There's always next time.'

'That's what Clive said.'

Outside the shop they hugged briefly and separated. Hetty wandered back up the street. Outside the second-hand bookshop she hesitated. Then, because she always found second-hand bookshops — and Philip's in particular — irresistible, she went inside.

'Hello, Hetty. You look warm and lavishly laden. Come and sit down. Have a drink?' Philip Gerard took her parcels from her and pulled out a chair.

'I'd love a glass of water.'

He made a face. 'I was about to offer you chilled wine. Have water, if you must.'

'It's a lovely idea, but I have work to do this afternoon and I'd probably go to sleep.'

Gerard laughed. 'Wise woman. Have dinner with me instead?'

Hetty's eyes widened. They had never been on eating-together terms before. 'All right,' she agreed, and smiled seductively. 'Where?'

'Goodness.' He sounded half-startled, half-pleased. Apparently the pleasure had the ascendancy for he continued shyly, 'I thought you'd say no. But there's a great little pub on the way to Abergavenny. Would you like to try it?'

Two offers to dinner in two days. Hetty's mind reeled. 'Great,' she said. 'That water you offered me?' When he had fetched it she said, 'I didn't come in for either water or a dinner invitation.'

'You want to buy a book as well?'

'A copy of Keats, please.'

'Correct me if I'm wrong, but haven't I already sold you one of those?'

'It's a long story but I gave it away.'

'Handsome present. I think I've only got a fairly mundane edition at the moment. I could look out for something a bit classier, if you are treating yourself.'

They discussed prices. Another customer entered and began browsing. After settling on a time for Philip to pick her up, Hetty left.

Hetty had known Philip Gerard for many years. The shop had sold second-hand books for as long as anyone could remember. When the previous owner decided to retire, he advertised the business with its goodwill and Philip Gerard duly arrived in Otterhaven. He appeared to have no family and word had it that he had left London to get over an affair that had gone sadly wrong. Whatever the truth of that rumour, Philip neither dismissed nor verified it. There were some now who were convinced that he was gay. Hetty could not bring herself to be bothered either way. She thought of Philip Gerard as her friend. There were things she had confided in him — mainly concerning school — that she had not mentioned to anyone else for, gay or not, she trusted his discretion totally. This invitation, though, was a puzzle.

★ ★ ★

Later that evening they were at a table by an open window overlooking a charming court-yard filled with roses that scented the air and with a fountain nearby that flowed musically over cobbles. Hetty, wearing the new spotted navy linen which Philip had already compli-mented her on, put down her glass of red wine and asked frankly, 'Is there any particular reason why you asked me out tonight?'

'You look delightful. You are a charming dinner companion. What more could a man want?'

'You don't actually know what sort of a companion I am, though. Previously our encounters have always been confined to the shop.'

'Dear, you make it sound too, too boring for words.'

'Be sensible. Is it something I should know or something you want to tell me?'

'Does it have to be anything special?' he countered defensively.

'I suppose not. I'm just surprised, that's all.

And I know you well enough to say that.'

'Perhaps it's just that you're a good customer.'

Hetty picked up her steak knife. 'I do hope you are going to be serious,' she said sternly.

'I intended to be serious, but not until after we'd eaten. I didn't want to spoil your digestion.'

'Now you really have me worried.'

It was Clive Makepeace, she was thinking. Philip was warning her off. Or was it Tom Gillard? How complicated her life had become!

Philip cleared his throat. 'What would you say if I told you I have fallen in love?' At the look on her face he gave a great guffaw, which caused several of the other diners to turn in their direction. 'I'm sorry, Hetty. But if you could just see your face . . . '

Hetty finished chewing on her steak, which was quite deliciously tender, in order to give herself time to reply. It isn't me, she was thinking, her feelings compounded of relief (she liked Philip very much, but live with him, become intimate with him?) and chagrin (after what had been happening to her recently it was not so out of the question that she should receive a proposal, was it?). And that, Hetty Loveridge, has to be considered soberly on another occasion, she thought.

'I'm glad you find my reaction so amusing,' she said tartly. 'It's just the last thing I expected to hear you say.'

Then she put down her knife and fork and lent across to take Philip's hand. 'I hope I am to be happy for you,' she went on gently. 'Is this why you wanted to tell me in private?'

'I wouldn't exactly call this private.'

'Someone always comes into the shop. Which is as it should be. So, go on. Who is this lucky lover?'

'How tactful you are, Hetty. Not mentioning the pronouns he or she. It's a he, of course.'

'Of course.'

'You aren't shocked?'

'In this day and age? My only amazement is that it's taken you so long to find someone special.'

Philip shrugged. 'I was happier on my own after the debacle of my earlier liaison. I've had the odd moment, in London, where no one knows me . . . '

'Dangerous,' she commented.

'Quite so. Karl and I met by chance at a book fair six months ago. The thing is . . . ' He hesitated for so long, Hetty knew what was coming. 'The thing is, Karl has had AIDS diagnosed.'

'Oh, Philip . . . Not you, also?'

189

'Heavens, no.' She noticed he sounded appalled. 'Do you think that is the reaction everyone'll have?'

Hetty shook her head. 'I don't know. If they do, it will be in sympathy with you, not revulsion. At least, not among your friends.'

'I guess I'll know who they are, soon enough.'

'Are you leaving Otterhaven?'

'Certainly not. You see, that's the whole point. Next week Karl is coming to live with me. That's the first hurdle, people discovering my orientation. The AIDS part won't come into it for some time because at the moment Karl is in remission. Who knows how long that will last? But I wanted to test the waters with someone I thought, hoped, I could rely on. You. That's why I asked you out to dinner, Hetty. Do you want me to take you home straight away?'

'There's another glass of wine left in the bottle,' she said evenly, 'though I won't have any pudding. But don't let that stop you. The choices look just as good as the other courses.'

'I'm going to have a brandy.'

'In that case why don't we go back to my place so you can walk home afterwards?'

'So sensible, Hetty. And quite right too. Drink-driving would finish the business.'

She caught hold of his hand for the second time that evening. 'I'm really glad you have found someone at last. You must have been a lonely man for a very long time.'

'Do you know, it was seeing the change in you that gave me the courage to propose to Karl that we should live together, and I do mean as a couple.'

She registered that with interest. Then she said, 'The change in me? I don't understand.'

'That mother of yours. No, don't interrupt, Hetty. Everyone knew how difficult she made your life. Everyone has always admired you so for the way in which you coped with her.'

Hetty said fiercely, 'My mother never made my life difficult. If anyone did it was I, myself.'

'If you say so.' He looked at her narrowly. 'On the other hand, you cannot deny that since her death you have blossomed.'

Once again Hetty echoed his words. 'Blossomed! Whatever do you mean, Philip Gerard?'

'That dress. Tom Gillard. Dinner last night with Clive Makepeace.'

'How do you know about last night?'

He noticed she said nothing about Tom Gillard. 'News travels in Otterhaven. You know that.'

'Dreadful village gossips.'

'And you wouldn't have it any other way.'

'No one has gossiped about me before.' She stopped. 'Do you mean to tell me I've been the subject of gossip all these years without knowing it?'

'Of course you have. In the nicest possible way, naturally.' He took back his cheque card and left a generous tip. 'Come on, I'll take you home and you can pour me a large brandy while we speculate what the gossip will be after tonight.'

It was as she said good night, very much later, kissing Philip on the cheek, that Hetty said, 'It was two dresses I bought this morning. I thought you might like to know.'

⋆   ⋆   ⋆

It was a week after Megan had gone to visit her aunt and uncle. There had been no word from Tom Gillard. Ah, well, Hetty had thought philosophically, a relationship with Tom Gillard would not have been an easy ride. It was best forgotten, whatever there had already been between them, that she had ever contemplated there might possibly be a relationship.

There was, however, her promise to Tom's daughter that she would get in touch with Jit Singh.

Before she left Otterhaven, Megan had made sure that Hetty had Jit's mobile number.

'Though if she's changed it, I'm not sure what you do then.'

'Surely people don't change their mobiles without making sure their friends have the new number?' objected Hetty, who had only very recently bought her first, her mother considering their invention to have been inspired by the devil himself. 'But I do remember the Singhs' address so I could always write to her.'

'Snail mail!'

'Don't worry. I'll be in touch with Jit, as I promised, and then I'll relay whatever news I have of Balbiro to you through your father.' Hetty supposed that she could rely on Tom to pass on whatever news she had to Megan but she thought it would be better not to voice her fears that he might think it kinder to leave his daughter in ignorance. Which thought presupposed that the news was unlikely to be good news. Oh dear, thought Hetty, why do I have this feeling of doom?

In the event, Jit had not changed her mobile and she answered it at once when Hetty kept her promise. Jit sounded guarded, but pleased that Hetty had contacted her.

'Miss Loveridge,' she said abruptly, when

Hetty was about to ring off, almost as though quite suddenly she was able to speak freely, 'do you think I might come and see you?'

'Of course, dear,' said Hetty, who was startled by the request, but intrigued at the same time. 'When would you like to come?'

They settled on the Sunday afternoon.

'How will you get here?'

'My husband, Sobha, will drive me.'

That answered one of the questions Hetty wanted answering. Jit was still with her husband. Something at least had been salvaged from the disastrous wedding day. What had not, she would learn soon enough.

# 10

Saturday morning saw Hetty at The Grange again. It was a beautiful morning, fresh with a promise of heat to come once the sun had burnt off a residual mist. As Tom was not there, Clive set her to help Sheila, who was working in the middle of the walled garden. A large rectangular bed had already been cleared of weeds and rough dug. Inside this rectangle were marked four squares with a circle in the centre of the rectangle. This was the planned knot garden.

'There will be a fountain in the centre, if we ever have enough money for it. Otherwise I guess we shall just have to make do with a statue,' said Sheila. In one of the squares Sheila had begun pegging out a complicated pattern with thin rope. 'It's based on a Celtic knot,' she informed Hetty. 'Take these pegs, will you, and we'll see if we can make sense of it. Do you draw or sew or anything? If you do, you will understand more easily how the lines go over then under each other.'

Hetty confessed an ignorance on the subject of Celtic knots, but once she had traced with her finger one of the lines on the template Sheila was holding, she saw what had to be done.

'Complicated,' she said. 'How long do we have?'

'As long as it takes. The ground has been dug but we shall be treading on it now, so each line will have to be prepared properly for the box hedging to be planted at a later date. Clive is thinking end of September for the hedging so that it can settle for the winter, but we won't be planting the herbs until the spring.'

They spent a satisfying morning with the rope and the pegs, and by the time they had finished the outer rectangle and two of the squares had been completed. Sheila observed that it would not take nearly so long the following week provided they worked together. It seemed to be assumed that Hetty would be there weekly and as Hetty had enjoyed working with Sheila she did not demur.

Sheila mentioned their progress enthusiastically to Clive as they were all putting their tools away. 'Hetty got to understand the knot far quicker than I did.'

Clive accompanied Hetty to her car. 'You will help Sheila next week, won't you?' he asked anxiously. 'Only she is quite right. Something like that can take hours if you

196

don't know what you are doing.'

'I'll be here,' promised Hetty. Clive was hovering. 'I have to go now. I said I'd help Mary strip lavender this afternoon and I need to eat a sandwich and get cleaned up first.'

'Care to have dinner with me this evening?' he asked, not looking at her, but scuffing at the gravel with his toe.

Like a small boy who isn't quite convinced he'd get the answer he wanted, Hetty thought indulgently.

'I'd have liked that,' she answered gently. 'But Mary has asked me to stay on and have supper with the family.'

'Oh. Well, I suppose I can't compete with the castle,' he said. 'Are you meeting up later with your new friend?'

There was an unpleasant timbre to his voice. Hetty's eyebrows rose a fraction. 'My new friend? I'm not sure who you mean.'

'That bookseller chappie. Gerard, or whatever his name is. Absolute poofter, I've always thought.'

'I've known Philip Gerard since he first came to Otterhaven,' Hetty said coldly. 'I always buy my books from him. He is a very good friend in the best sense of that word and I'd like you to remember that.'

'So you always kiss your very good friends good night?' he demanded.

197

Hetty looked Clive squarely in his face, which had become livid with an emotion she recognized immediately. Good Lord, she thought, he's jealous. Clive Makepeace is jealous of Philip Gerard on my account. She felt like laughing at the absurdity of the notion — that anyone could experience envy as a result of anything she might or might not have done. But this needed stamping on straight away. In a clipped voice she said, 'Either you were watching, in which case you would have seen that what passed between us was a simple expression of friendship, or you have listened to gossip, which in this case is malicious. Whatever, it is absolutely none of your business and I really don't care for any of your insinuations.'

She wondered, then, if there had been a hidden agenda behind Philip's invitation to dinner. Had she been primed to be his ambassador? Was this her mission now? And if so, did she want it? Should she tell Clive that Philip's special 'friend' was due to arrive in Otterhaven any day now, confirming his suspicions as to Philip's sexual orientation? Certainly not, she concluded. It was neither here nor there what Clive thought of Philip Gerard. Though that wasn't true, either. It mattered to her. It concerned her because Philip was a friend and as such she would stand by him both at this time and in times to come. It also proved to her that there were facets to Clive's character that it was just as well she was discovering.

Clive did not bluster. He sagged. 'I-I didn't . . . I-I wasn't. I wouldn't offend you for anything, Hetty.'

Hetty thought she could actually see water glistening in his eyes as they took on an abject, doggy appeal. 'Then please be very careful what you say about me and my friends in the future.'

'But there is to be a future, with us?'

'I don't think there would ever be an 'us', Clive,' Hetty replied. But she spoke more kindly this time. It was apparent that the man's ego was easily bruised. That there could never be a so-called future with him was one thing. Given the trauma he had suffered, Hetty did not want to shatter the man's confidence unnecessarily.

'But we could meet occasionally?'

'We have met this morning.'

'I meant socially. Like in go out together?'

Hetty felt she had been manipulated. Taking on work at The Grange was the most agreeable way of volunteering she could imagine. She had very much enjoyed her morning with Sheila. She did not want to alienate Clive because if there were an atmosphere between them she might decide that she would have to leave.

'We could go for a drink sometime, I suppose,' she said grudgingly.

'I'd like that very much. Wednesday?'

Ensnared, Hetty agreed. But she did so hope another woman would take Clive's fancy, and very soon.

★   ★   ★

'What have you done with your husband?' Hetty asked when she opened the door on Sunday afternoon to find Jit standing there on her own. She had been expecting to see Sobha Singh with the girl and she had not been too sure how she and Jit would be able to have a personal talk with him sitting beside them.

'I sent him to look round the village,' Jit answered, stepping into the cottage. She was elegantly dressed in a *shalwar kameez* in a pale blue silk decorated with gold embroidery, high-heeled open-backed sandals, and her bracelets, earrings and a necklace were a delicately wrought gold.

Hetty kissed her impulsively and was pleased that Jit hugged her in return. 'I hope he won't be too bored. Is he coming back for tea?'

'No. I told Sobha he could pick me up at five. I brought these for you,' she added shyly, handing Hetty a bunch of pink carnations. 'Though I had forgotten you have a garden. They are probably superfluous.'

'Not at all. I love the perfume and I don't grow them myself. Anyway, even if I did I wouldn't cut them for the house. Thank you so very much. Come through into the garden, dear. It's quite sheltered out there.' She settled the girl into a comfortable chair. 'I'll put the flowers in water and make the tea in a minute. How are you, Jit? Is everything all right with you? I do hope you don't mind that I telephoned, but I promised Megan that I'd keep in touch. You did know that Megan has gone to France with an aunt and uncle?'

'Of course. I wondered why she . . . Megan did tell me. I forgot.'

'And Balbiro? Has she come home?' That was the most important question. Hetty thought she might just as well ask it immediately though she had a shrewd suspicion that the reason why Jit had asked to visit her had to be something to do with her cousin.

'Balbiro is still missing,' Jit said. Her face was impassive. 'No one has the least idea, even now, what has happened to her.'

'I'll make the tea, then you can tell me all about it.'

Hetty put on the kettle and found a vase for the carnations, which she placed on a side table in the sitting-room. Then she made the tea, fetched egg and cress sandwiches and a jam sponge cake from her pantry and carried the tray out into the garden. Jit was sitting where she had left her. There was a quality of stillness about her that Hetty did not remember from her schooldays, as if she were very much aware of her surroundings, wary of what might be asked of her but prepared for the decisions that she would have to make. Hetty was not sure how she knew this but she was certain that she was right.

The tea poured, Jit began her story. Resham was distraught after the wedding, she told Hetty. He could not believe that the day which had started so auspiciously could have ended in such ruin. His reaction had come as a surprise to Balbiro's family, but apparently Resham had thought of the marriage as a love match all along and that was why he was so horrified that she had gone.

'Why Resham didn't tell her he loved her no one will ever know,' Jit said soberly. 'If only he had. He keeps saying that himself. He thought his father had made it clear to my uncle that the suggestion that he and Balbiro should marry was something he very much wanted. Apparently all that was said was that Balbiro would be made most welcome in their family.'

'A very prosaic way of putting it,' agreed Hetty. 'Perhaps Resham's father thought reticence was preferable. Perhaps he thought that Balbiro, not to mention her family, might be put off the match if he confessed his son loved her.'

'But Miss Loveridge, how was Balbiro to guess that Resham was in love with her?'

'How indeed?'

'Balbiro always wanted a love match. She said so, many times.'

'Surely she must have had some clue? I mean, I know it is not always considered proper for a young Indian couple to spend much time alone, but surely she must have had an inkling that what Resham was offering her was not merely an arranged marriage?'

'Resham himself insisted that they should do the whole thing properly. I think he had some romantic notion of telling Balbiro how much she meant to him on their wedding night.'

'So sad, this lack of communication. Then, it is the running away a second time that I find difficult to fathom.' Hetty voiced her perplexity. 'I mean, I do understand that running away to stay with Megan was bad enough, especially once it was known that Megan's brother had come home unexpectedly, but Megan explained how that had come about satisfactorily, didn't she, so why run away once the marriage had taken place?'

'I s'pose she thought that by then it was too late. The damage was done. The gossip had already spread.'

'What has happened since?'

'Resham was adamant that however much it cost, our families should consult a firm that specializes in finding Indian girls who have run away. He said there was to be no force but that the private investigator was to make sure Balbiro understood that no one blamed her for running away, that she must come home to him.'

'And . . . ?'

'Balbiro seems to have disappeared off the face of the earth. There is another thing. Keval, Balbiro's brother, has gone, too.'

'He has disappeared also?'

'Keval hasn't disappeared, exactly, though they haven't yet got an address for him,' Jit said. Her eyes were troubled and her answer hesitant, as if she did not want to have to expose the families' trauma to someone who was little better than a stranger, but who felt nevertheless that she had no option. 'Keval announced a few days ago that he was going back to Punjab. He was to catch a flight that very evening. My auntie and uncle are out of their minds with worry.'

'Do you know why he has gone?'

'He says this country is corrupt, that society here is evil.'

'Has he always felt this way?'

'Oh, no. When he was at school he was into everything. You know, he loved the fashions and the pop charts. He had all the best singles.'

'Then he changed?' Hetty prompted her.

'It happened about a year ago, Balbiro told me. He stopped going out, except to the *Gurdwara*. He began to read a lot about India, the Sikhs. At first he was very much against Resham marrying his sister, though they had once been best friends. Then I think he was just glad she was marrying as the family wanted. And now he says it is impossible for him to remain here. The only way he can live is by going back to his roots.'

'I thought he was second generation British. You were all born in this country, were you not?'

'That is so. Keval was born in Shepherd's Bush.'

Jit hesitated for a moment and Hetty filled the quiet by offering her more tea and

205

another sandwich. She thought she knew what the girl was going to say. This was yet one more example of the disaffection felt by a young man who found himself unable to appreciate all that his parents had sought to gain by leaving their own place and settling in another country. It did not seem to matter to this new generation whether their parents had left for asylum or whether they had managed to relocate for economic reasons. These young men appeared to consider themselves bereft of the certainties of their own culture. (Why was this confined to young men? Was it because young women were more in tune with the realities of life, or was it because they were not able to put rebellion into practice? It was something she would like to think about later.) Of course, Keval was not like the Muslim suicide bombers who had wreaked so much devastating havoc, young men with no job, living on benefits (some of them — did that unman them?). Keval was not a Muslim. And he had a job.

'It is not quite the same with my people as it is with the Muslims,' said Jit, echoing Hetty's thoughts, 'but a lot of our young men dislike the way of life here. They long for the assurances of life as it is at home.'

'Oh, Jit, even you call it home.'

'I was quoting,' she said indignantly.

'Sobha calls Punjab his home, of course. But if he ever tries to insist that I should return with him, I would not go. My parents took us to Punjab five years ago for a holiday and to meet our cousins. My brother married a second cousin, you know, and brought her over here. They seem happy enough. Anyway, I hated every minute of our visit: the poverty, the beggars. Did you know they deform their children deliberately to get more sympathy from the rich tourists? It's disgusting. Then there were the smells, the filth. I even disliked the food, would you believe that? I couldn't wait to get home.' There was no mistaking the ring of truth in her voice. 'My mother would go back tomorrow, if she had a plane ticket. But me?' Jit shook her head violently so that her gold earrings caught the sunlight and glinted.

Hetty thought wistfully that India was a country she had always longed to visit: to see the temples, the palaces, the mountains, yes, and even experience the dust, the dirt and the smells. Yet going to a country as a tourist was a very different thing from going there as one who was supposed to be familiar with conditions from an accident of birth. Tactfully, all she said was:

'And are you happy now?'

Jit's face said it all. By some extraordinary

chance — was it chance that had brought these two together? — Jit had discovered in her husband most of the qualities for which she had hoped. Not to put too fine a point on it, she had fallen in love with the man her parents had urged her to marry. And the young man, thought Hetty, not able to ask that question of Jit, what of him? Gradually the picture of the young couple emerged. It seemed that Sobha was very pleased with his lot. As well he might be, again thought Hetty. Sobha's English was already quite fluent and since he had learnt to drive some years before, he had recently been given a car.

'I am learning to drive, too. I have my L plates and I drove us here,' Jit said proudly. 'Sobha says that we will buy a small car for me once I have passed my test.' She told Hetty then that Sobha had given up the garden furniture factory immediately after their marriage and, having decided that accountancy bored him, had found a job working for a Sikh import/export firm in Cardiff. In spite of his rejecting the family firm, her parents had found them a small house in Cardiff into which they were to move the following week.

'Cardiff,' said Hetty. 'I had imagined you would want to settle near your parents.'

Jit shrugged. 'There was no proper work

for Sobha in Chepstow. Myself, I am glad to get away. Cardiff is an exciting city.'

Hetty was reminded of Megan, of the friendship that had grown between the two young women. It was only natural that both would want the freedom of new surroundings — even if for one of them it included the restrictions of a marriage.

'Miss Loveridge,' said Jit, leaning forward earnestly. 'There is one thing you could do for me and this is the reason — one of the reasons — I am so glad to see you this afternoon. You see, if it had not been for Balbiro disappearing, I think I would have done exactly what everyone expected of me. I should have settled happily as Sobha's wife, become pregnant almost immediately and started a family. But things have changed. I want to go to uni as we planned.'

Hetty's eyes widened. 'But I thought you had already turned down your place. Of course, it was Cardiff, wasn't it?' This was interesting. She looked at Jit with a dawning respect. Here was no meek Indian girl who was prepared to subsume her interests in those of her new husband. This was a girl who intended taking every advantage her intellect had already given her.

'I never wrote to Cardiff. I just left things as they were. But the results are coming out this week and provided my grades are satisfactory the next thing for me to do is to accept the offered place, innit? My parents wouldn't know what has to be done and neither will Sobha. I should like to be able to come to you for advice.'

'What does Sobha have to say to all this?'

'You do understand that I am happy with this marriage? I knew it would have to happen one day, and I think my parents made a good choice for me, but I am not yet nineteen. I am not prepared to become pregnant and bear several children and then have nothing to do for the rest of my life but look after them and a house and garden. I want to get myself a qualification. Maybe when I am twenty-five I shall be happy to start a family, to take a break in my career.' Jit smiled broadly for the first time. 'Did you get that? Take a break in my career?'

Hetty smiled back. 'It sounds great. Does Sobha agree to all this?'

'I think he was a little surprised.'

That was putting it mildly, Hetty thought. She wondered how long the row had lasted. Then she thought that maybe there had been no row. After all, Sobha Singh had everything he wanted. He could afford to be complaisant about a wife who did not conform to the expected Sikh norm.

'But Sobha agrees that this is what I should do. He has promised that he will not mention going back to Punjab until I am fully qualified. I think he believes that by then I will have changed my mind. But I won't. If he wants to return he will have to return alone.'

Control, Hetty was thinking. This was what Jit had accomplished: the control of her own life. If Balbiro had become the happy wife of a childhood friend, it was likely that Jit would never have had the courage to rebel, to be different. With the truly awful consequences of malicious gossip before her, she had determined not to become another victim. (Was Balbiro a victim, or had she also taken her life under her own control? Would they ever find out?)

'When will you tell your parents about your plans?' Hetty asked.

'Not until everything has been settled. Once I have accepted the place and everything has been arranged, then I shall tell them. They won't like it, I know that.'

'Your parents might dumbfound you. They might be very proud that you have the initiative to do something you very much desire.'

The doorbell rang. It was Sobha Singh, prompt to the minute. They said their goodbyes, Jit promising to be in touch after the results were published. Hetty watched them walk towards their car. The young man seemed caring, protective. Whatever happened to them over the next few days, months and years, Hetty hoped she would be allowed to see it.

★   ★   ★

It was not until lunchtime on Tuesday that Tom Gillard contacted her.

'I gather you have news about Balbiro for Megan. I'm sorry I wasn't here when you phoned. I've been running a painting workshop in Pembrokeshire.'

'You'd better tell Megan that the news is the same as it was,' said Hetty regretfully. 'Pembrokeshire sounds good, though.'

'Look, why don't we catch up over dinner?'

'I'd like that,' said Hetty warmly. 'When do you suggest?'

As he was busy that night (out with another woman? wondered Hetty, and reminded herself that this was the very attitude she had criticized in Clive), and she was having a drink with that same man on the Wednesday, they settled on Thursday, Tom insisting that he should cook for her.

'The exam results will be out by then. Are

you coming to the school for them on Megan's behalf?'

'They are being e-mailed to her. She promised to phone me around lunchtime.'

'Then we shall definitely have some celebrating to do,' said Hetty. 'I'll bring a bottle, shall I?'

'Heavens, I do hope you're right about the results. Just bring yourself, Hetty. I've not decided what we'll eat.'

'Fine, but I am right, Tom. Trust me.'

★   ★   ★

Hetty was not a keen TV viewer (unlike her mother, who had been an avid follower of several soaps) and previously her evenings had been spent on her marking which, given the number of sixth-form pupils she taught, was time-consuming. But because her social life had been given such a lift recently, she decided she would have to work the next day on her preparations for the forthcoming school year. By Wednesday evening she felt she deserved a break.

Wearing her spotted linen, Hetty met Clive Makepeace in the bar of The Otter. The hour they spent together was entirely congenial, the awkwardness of the Saturday apparently having been set aside. The subjects they

213

covered began with seventeenth-century English literature, which Hetty admitted sadly wasn't taught any more.

'Do you mean to tell me that children nowadays leave school without knowing any Milton?'

She agreed that it was, indeed, a crime against civilization let alone creative writing. Clive said that nowadays he most admired the poetry of Wilfred Owen and Siegfried Sassoon. 'I don't care to get any more modern than that,' he said.

Tactfully, and because she disagreed with him, Hetty turned the subject to Clive's passion, the walled garden. 'You must have done a lot of reading on the subject.'

'Not only reading about walled gardens — I like to visit them when I can. It was always difficult when Ver . . . Well, anyway, I'm planning a week's holiday in September,' he told her. 'I'm going to stay near Hadrian's Wall and walk the middle section unless the weather is awful. There's also a garden there I've been wanting to see for ages. It's called Chesters Walled Garden and in it is a knot garden from a design dating back to 1617.'

'That sounds very interesting. Are you going on your own?' She stopped, knowing it was pejorative, wishing she had not said that. 'I mean, do you join a group of gardeners when you go on holiday?'

'I'm not really into group activities,' he said. 'I suppose you . . . No, you wouldn't, of course.'

She did not pretend to misunderstand him. 'Not really, Clive. Anyway, it would be impossible. Term starts at the beginning of September. Remember, I'm a working woman.'

It had been a pity about that gaffe, she thought, as she closed the front door behind Clive. He had insisted on escorting her to her door, though she had been very firm about not inviting him inside because she still had work to do. She had even permitted him to kiss her on the cheek — though she had deliberately not reciprocated, since she felt instinctively that if she gave him the slightest encouragement he would be a difficult man to shake off.

Drat it, she thought. Men are so tender in their susceptibilities. Women are much more robust.

She took off the spotted linen and hung it up, wishing she had thought to wear trousers and a cardi. She certainly wasn't going to wear that dress when she met Tom the next evening.

# 11

'I've got four A$^*$ grades, Miss Loveridge.'

It was the day the A level results came out.

Hetty always planned her summer so that she would be available for her students on that day. At school there would be deserved euphoria, outpourings of ecstatic relief, hugs and congratulations. Regrettably there would also be the downcast faces, the tears of disappointment as it became apparent that the work done for the exams had either not been sufficient or that the girl in question had been allowed to over-estimate her abilities (probably the fault of a career-minded parent, for the staff preferred to be realistic over these things).

This day was no exception. One of the first to rush over and hug her, her precious piece of paper flapping wildly in her hand, her face radiant, was Jit Singh.

'Dear, that's marvellous. Absolutely splendid. I do so congratulate you and now you must go and tell your family.'

'I shall.'

'And you will get in touch, if you need any support?'

216

Of course she would. Jit would let nothing get in her way now.

After the other congratulations and the few, unfortunate commiserations, there were practical things to be done: the successful needed to be reminded that their chosen university would be contacting them, having already been notified of the results several days before. A letter would be in the post for those with an unconditional offer so there was no need for them to clog the telephone lines. For the others there was sensible advice: get in touch with their university, find out if there might be a place after all if they were just one grade down. Provided the course was not over-subscribed, they might get an offer even now. For the unfortunates, now was the time to ask what they really wanted to do. Had they considered other options?

There were two more students about whom Hetty was particularly curious. Megan telephoned her at teatime to tell her she had the grades she needed, but that Jit had found out that Balbiro had barely scraped pass grades.

'I always knew you had it in you. What a shame about Balbiro.'

'I don't understand it. She was passionate about becoming a doctor. She so wanted to work with sick children. She said it was such

217

a waste that Mrs Singh had given up her work when she was married and she was determined it wouldn't happen to her.'

'Megan, did she say anything about this when she was staying at the cottage?' asked Hetty cautiously. 'I mean, did you talk about anything other than the marriage? Or do you think it is possible Balbiro just abandoned her studies once she knew her parents insisted that she got married?'

'Actually, we didn't talk about the marriage very much. I mean, like, I thought she needed space.'

Hetty considered that Megan had shown a touching thoughtfulness.

'Jit thought Balbiro was working hard right up to the last minute,' Megan continued. 'She did herself, and look at the results. She's even persuaded Sobha to allow her to go to uni.'

'I get the impression that would not have been the case for Balbiro.'

'I wonder if we'll ever know the truth,' said Megan, echoing suspicions that Hetty refused to contemplate for long; declining to confront the possibility that she would never return.

Hetty suspected, though, that once Balbiro knew that marriage was what her parents had chosen for her, she had more or less given up on her studies. Either that or she had been in such a turmoil that she had not been able to

218

study. Which was a pity because apparently she had an able mind. It was not that she blamed Balbiro's teachers for having failed to realize there was a problem — after all, both Jit and Balbiro had kept their impending marriages a secret until the end of term. It was just that this was yet another disappointment with which the girl must cope — when eventually she returned to her family.

Balbiro's Journal, 29th July

My parents had begun to think that everything was going to be fine. All the preparations for the day of the marriage were in order and still no one had mentioned anything about my disappearance.

I think I always knew it was too good to be true. I mean, who was I to think I had the right or the ability to change what had always been?

The morning of the wedding day I threw up almost as soon as I got out of bed. I was so scared even the thought of food made me nauseous and I was trembling so much that my mother got cross when she was helping me to dress.

'Anyone would think you were going to your execution,' she cried. 'Oh my God, you are pregnant, you dreadful girl! Keval was right all along, wasn't he? It is that man, Megan's brother. It happened when you ran away. Don't lie to me, your mother.'

I could see it was only with difficulty that she

stopped herself from slapping me yet again (afraid the marks would show).

'Nothing happened, Ma,' I said, retching away. 'I told you. I am a virgin.'

(I am just scared, I wanted to say. I wanted to be comforted. But I couldn't say any of that.)

When we got to the Gurdwara I could see that Mrs Cooper was concerned about me. Nosey old cow. No, I suppose that isn't fair. I have always got on with her. She gave Keval and me Christmas presents while we were still at school and she'd already sent me a cheque for a wedding present. But she told Miss Loveridge that I didn't seem well. So that meant there were two who were examining me closely as though I was an insect.

Resham did look fine. I was very proud of him.

I wish he had noticed me. Really noticed me, I mean. I don't believe he looked at me once.

He is a fine man. He has a good job and excellent prospects. I expect he deserves better than me for his wife. It wouldn't matter to me what he is worth or how he looks for I have always loved him.

That is something I shall never tell him.

But I took the end of the scarf only a second after Jit and the wedding was concluded.

It all happened so quickly after that. There were whispers. Faces were turned in my direction. At first I thought it was imagination, brought about by my certainty that something would go wrong.

Keval strode towards us. He tore me from Resham's side. He dragged me into the garden.

'They are knowing that you ran away. They are saying that you ran away to meet an English boy. They are saying you cannot possibly be a virgin. Resham's family will have to repudiate you. You have ruined us.'

I can't write any more now. My eyes are too full of tears . . .

Changing out of an old skirt that evening, Hetty's hand hovered over a flowered cotton skirt that she had always thought was pretty, but now thought it looked decidedly faded. She regarded the two new dresses doubtfully, took down the skirt from its hanger and put that on with its red short-sleeved top. She was halfway downstairs before she turned and went back to her bedroom, stepped out of the skirt and took off the top and reached for the spotted linen. She thought to herself as she hung the skirt on its hanger again that at her age she really should have more sense than to dither over clothes. Still, she went into her mother's room and looked critically at her reflection in the long mirror in the now empty wardrobe. The dress suited her. Hetty smiled at herself; then she frowned.

Why had she never insisted that she needed a long mirror in her own room? Ever since she had taken an interest in how she appeared (seven, eight?) she had been forced to enter her mother's bedroom to look at herself in the long mirror. Inevitably her mother had some comment to make, for she was always present, which involved some subtle change in the effect Hetty had been trying to achieve, gentle though the comment might be.

'Your knees aren't your best feature, are they, dear?' — when skirts were fashionably short.

'Don't you think those trousers are a little . . . tight?'

'Are you trying to tell me my bum looks fat in this?'

'Such a crude way of putting it.'

Hetty never wore jeans again which was crazy, now she came to think about it, because nowadays there were so many brands to choose from: hip slimming, leg lengthening, bum reducing.

Latterly the criticism had been more along the lines of: 'Real pearls look so much glossier than cheap ones.' Though admittedly that observation had been followed by: 'You could always borrow mine . . . '

Hetty put her head on one side and considered the bedroom carefully. For the first time since her mother had died that was what it had become: a bedroom. It had taken a gritty determination for Hetty to strip her mother's room of its identity. She had only been able to do it by playing Classic FM very loudly — as if to drown out Joan's protests? Hetty smiled at the whimsy. Yet she had succeeded. Now the room was nothing more than that: an empty bedroom.

It did need, however, a new carpet — and the curtains were heavy and dull. But this room was larger and airier than her own. It had ample storage space (and the long mirror) and the furniture, if not antique, was solid and substantial without making the interior seem smaller. It was ridiculous that she had not thought to use it herself, that she was still sleeping in her old, childhood, room. She resolved that the very next day she would begin to redecorate and claim it for herself.

A new bed, Hetty thought. That was what she would also buy for herself. On second thoughts she would keep the bedstead because, like the dressing-table, it was rosewood. But the mattress sagged (as did her own). She would buy a mattress that was supremely comfortable — and one that would give proper support for an ageing back. She would give herself permission to be both extravagant and practical at the same time. She thought she might even boast of this to Polly Firmer the next time she saw her.

Hetty was still smiling as she parked the car in Tom Gillard's drive.

'You look cheerful,' he said, opening her door and in his eyes she saw ample justification for the spotted linen. He had come out immediately he saw her turn into the drive and waited while she parked the car neatly.

'I've just decided to buy myself a new mattress,' Hetty said.

'That's nice,' said Tom noncommittally.

'Don't laugh,' said Hetty uncomfortably, cursing the impulse that had made her mention anything so . . . intimate.

'Dear Hetty, of course I'm not laughing,' he said, and laughed. 'What on earth brought on this whim?'

Nothing would induce her to mention the long mirror. 'I went into my mother's room and realized how very much more spacious it is than my own, and the furniture is better.'

'Except for the bed.'

'The bed is fine. The mattress has seen better days.'

'As have we all. Go to a bed specialist, not just the nearest cheap furniture outlet. That's what I did a year back and the result is bliss.'

It was the strangest conversation. Though Tom had stopped laughing and was plainly trying to give her sensible advice.

224

'Don't forget to lie on the mattress and wriggle a bit before you decide to buy,' he said. 'And run from any shop assistant who objects.'

The smile in his eyes was still there — Hetty knew that Tom's smile reached his eyes with the slightest provocation. She was waiting warily for him to offer to show her his new bed. Before he succumbed to a temptation it was her own fault to have lain at his feet, she said hurriedly, 'You've heard from Megan, of course?'

'She phoned at teatime. Isn't it good news?' He positively beamed.

'I'm so glad for her.' They discussed practicalities as they went indoors and Tom poured her a glass of white wine.

'What I really wanted to tell you about was the Singh cousins.' Whatever the niceties of language and culture, Hetty used the surname, that had been assumed by the school.

'Balbiro has been found?'

Hetty shook her head slowly. There was a pause.

Tom put food on the table. 'I hope you don't mind eating in the kitchen? It's a fish pie. Simple food. I hope you like it. There's a salad and raspberries from the garden. I don't grow vegetables, but I have a gooseberry bush which my neighbour plunders and gives me jam in return and I keep the raspberries going.'

Hetty assured him that it all sounded delicious. Towards the end of the fish pie she returned to the news she wanted to give him about Jit. 'It was such a surprise. I can't tell you how glad I am that the girl's schooling won't be wasted.'

'I thought you were one of those who always insists that no education is ever wasted. Excuse me.' Tom pushed his chair back with such force it rocked on its legs. He rose and left the table abruptly, going out of the room and shutting the door behind him. She could hear his footsteps pounding upstairs; the door to the bathroom close with force.

He was gone for some time. Hetty finished her fish pie and sat quietly. When Tom eventually returned she regarded him with slightly raised eyebrows, but without uttering a word. His face was pale, though she thought she could see a glimmer of moisture in his eyes. For some reason this did not fill her with the repugnance that the same sight had induced in her from Clive Makepeace's face. It was not pity, either, but concern and a desire to make it better for Tom.

'You have a quality of silence that is

refreshing,' Tom said simply.

Hetty said nothing.

Tom picked up his fork, looked at the congealing food on his plate with distaste and got up, removing both plates.

'You could always warm it in the microwave,' she suggested softly.

'Lost my appetite.'

He scraped his plate, his back to her. When he returned to the table, Hetty could see that his face had lost a little of the pallor but his eyes were quite red. Without saying a word she reached out to take his hand as he put a carton of cream and a sugar sifter on to the table.

Then Tom sighed and sat down. He did not pull his hand away.

'Do you know what has been in the back of my mind ever since this awful debacle with the Singhs? I was convinced that once she knew that Jit was not going to take up her place in Cardiff, Meg would get it into her mind that she could take a year off.'

'Students do that, you know,' Hetty observed cautiously. 'Some people think it's good for them, girls as well as boys, to have a year out. Makes them grow up. You know, lets them get freedom out of their system so that they are ready to appreciate the opportunities university offers.'

'Do you think that, Hetty?'

Hetty shrugged. 'I think it depends on the individual student. I gather you think differently.'

'Only about Meg. I had this . . . abject fear that Meg would take off — not for any sense of adventure or a desire to travel but just to search for Balbiro. I was positive that I was about to lose her, as I lost her mother.'

Hetty's heart jolted. Any idiotically juvenile notions she had harboured about a romantic attachment with this man were firmly confounded at that moment. This was a man who was still as in love with his wife as he had ever been. It said a lot for his constancy, but very little for any future she might have in his life, other than as a friend. Then, wasn't it plain that it was a friend that Tom needed more than anything?

Tom must have seen something of how she felt in her face for he said, 'No, let me rephrase that. I got over the loss of Meg's mother a long time ago. I was being totally selfish, imagining how I would feel left on my own, for even Jake has his own life now. See what a fool I am.'

'Tom,' she said hesitantly, 'when Megan goes to university she is leaving home, you know. You can't expect to hold on to her for ever.'

He looked at her, almost disdainfully. 'I know that. But there is a world of difference between a girl who returns from a term at university and one who has sought the length and breadth of the country to find another who does not want to be found.'

He sounded as though he did not believe that Balbiro would ever be found. It almost seemed as though Tom thought that Balbiro was dead. It was the very first time that Hetty had voiced that notion, even silently. She shied away from it immediately. There were so many places the girl could have gone. Even without qualifications there were so many jobs she might have found that would have kept her housed, fed and clothed. (Not in Indian dress?) She could have gone to a woman's refuge. It was highly likely that an investigator would not have been given access to one of those. Or was it? They (whoever they were) would use a woman for that job. Balbiro could have become a mother's help; cut her hair or bought a wig and found a job in a supermarket. She could have turned to help from someone without scruples and found herself in a brothel . . . Some of this she explained haltingly to Tom.

'The sex-slave trade,' she ended quietly.

'And don't you think that is why I have

been so scared rotten for my daughter?' he said harshly.

'Tom, it wouldn't have happened like that . . .'

'Because Meg has more sense. Come off it, Hetty, things happen even to sensible girls, if they have what they consider is a mission. You read about it almost every day.'

'You read the most peculiar newspapers,' Hetty said tartly, thinking that this conversation was becoming altogether too morbid.

Tom laughed shakily and helped himself to a spoonful of raspberries, shaking a considerable amount of sugar on to them, but eschewing the cream. Hetty thought he probably needed the sugar.

They ate in silence for a time.

'Tea, coffee?' he asked. 'Or another glass of wine?'

'I think I'd better have another glass of plain water since I have to drive home,' Hetty said regretfully. At that moment she was not sure whether the regret was for not having the glass of wine or the idea of going home alone. Leaving Tom to face the night on his own?

Tom got up. To her surprise, when he came back to the table it was with another bottle of wine. 'Water, if you prefer,' he said, 'but don't drive home. I'd really like you to stay, Hetty. I don't want to be on my own tonight.'

There was no hesitation in her. Hetty accepted another glass of wine — and a large glass of water, knowing that it would help to flush the alcohol from her system. The question of the spare room — Tom's new mattress? — seemed irrelevant.

'Now that you've told me that Jit is going to take up her university place you just can't imagine the relief. Meg will go to university with her, even if Balbiro isn't around to be with them.' They were in the sitting-room, on comfortable chairs which were placed for the stunning view across the valley where lights winked in the far distance as brightness slowly drained from the sky. With a pang, Hetty realized that though the days remained warm, the year was beginning its descent towards autumn.

There was a small table beside them. Tom refilled their glasses from the bottle there. 'I have been so tense, just waiting for catastrophe. You simply can't imagine. I thought I had failed in everything I wanted to do for her.'

Without a child of her own, Hetty could not imagine what had run through Tom's mind unendingly. Yet with her years of teaching she knew that this was an emotion all caring parents experience. 'You have to learn to let go,' she murmured.

'I know. And truly, I was prepared for that. I do understand that I could not expect to control Meg's life for ever. Nor would I want to. What would be the point of bringing up a clone of myself?'

Hetty started. Was that what she had permitted her mother to do, to clone herself? She shook her head. How much had she struggled against that very thing? The answer seemed to be not very much, given that she preferred a quiet life at home. But how had she permitted this to go on for so long? Was she a clone of her mother? Heaven forbid. Though they did say that most women became their mothers, eventually . . .

'What is it?'

'Nothing important. I was just speculating on how easy it is for a parent to clone a child.'

'Very difficult, I'd say — even thinking about Meg, I can say that. I imagine most children resist any attempt to mould them into a clone of whoever is the stronger parent. There must come a time when the new persona gains the ascendancy.'

'Oof. I guess that makes me a strong contender for the title of arrested developer of all time.'

'Nonsense,' he replied robustly, and yawned. 'You were a dutiful daughter who was so anxious to support her mother in her declining years that you forgot to take care of yourself. Hetty, you need nurturing, and I need a good night's sleep. Come to bed.'

★ ★ ★

They left the debris of the evening.

Hetty did not use the spare room.

Early in the morning she wondered sleepily at the ease of it all. They said sex was a bit like riding a bicycle. Once you learnt the skill you didn't forget it. Then, she reasoned, she had been right about Tom needing a friend. Their act of friendship had been both loving and sleep-inducing and from the element of laughter that had also gone with their accommodations for each other, she did not expect there to be the least embarrassment once they were both awake, at what had been so inevitable.

★ ★ ★

Some time later, when she woke fully, Hetty lay alone on the new mattress (it was blissful, as Tom had promised) and heard the small sounds of work in the kitchen. There was also a faint aroma of coffee. She sat up, then decided not to feel guilty and to take her time. There was a clean towelling robe at the

233

foot of the bed with a clean towel and a new toothbrush beside it. How considerate! Luxuriating in the space of Tom's bathroom, Hetty suppressed the image of other women using the robe. Other women? Tom was a consummate lover — friend? — but really, at his age if he had not been so, that would have been the outrage. She even deemed her own performance, rusty as it was, not wholly inadequate, judging from his reaction to her.

Hetty took a long shower then clad herself in the towelling robe and went downstairs towards the enticing mouth-watering smell of a cooked breakfast.

'Bacon,' she said. 'How very degenerate.'

Tom spluttered with laughter. 'I said you needed nurturing. Eggs with it? Tomatoes, mushrooms?'

'Is that really the time? No wonder I'm famished. I'll have it all.'

'Mm,' he said, meaningfully. 'I expect the exercise had something to do with it.'

Hetty actually blushed. 'Myself, I think it was drinking all that water.'

'Tea or coffee? Proper coffee is ready. Help yourself to fruit juice first. There's apple or orange.'

'I could . . . ' She stopped, pouring apple juice to cover the moment. Get used to this? Not the way to go, Hetty Loveridge, she said sternly to herself.

'I hope so,' said Tom smoothly as if she had said it aloud, and brought a platter of hot food, warm plates, toast and coffee to the table for them both. 'Are you busy today?'

'Not really. Nothing that couldn't wait until tomorrow. Why?'

'Meg will be home tomorrow. I thought we'd take the day off. Have some fun.'

'What do you mean by fun?' Hetty asked guardedly.

'Do you remember I said I'd take your art appreciation in hand? There's a small gallery recently opened which is showing some John Pipers. Prints, lithographs, that sort of thing. Signed limited editions. I thought I'd take you to have a look at them. Then maybe lunch somewhere?'

'I don't know anything about John Piper.'

'I know. Is that a yes or a no?'

'Definitely a yes. Though you're not suggesting I buy anything, are you, I hope?'

'That would be up to you, but these are collectors' items rather than a whim buy.'

'Meaning I couldn't afford one.'

'If you can afford a new bed you could afford a Piper print.'

'It's only a mattress I'm buying, but I probably couldn't afford a print. Anyway, provided we stop at my home for me to change first, I'd like to see them.'

'I think you look just fine as you are.'

'I think you might be biased. Also people would most certainly look askance if I entered any gallery wearing this.'

'What you were wearing yesterday was gorgeous.'

Hetty rewarded Tom with a beaming smile. 'The dress is creased,' she said cheerfully. 'Besides . . . ' Thinking of the new blue, she was going to say that she could go one better. Then she thought she'd surprise him. 'I need clean underwear,' she said, and smiled even more broadly.

# 12

The Piper exhibition was housed in a small, cluttered room, part of a craft complex in converted stables.

'You don't really get to see them at their best here,' said Tom, 'but any chance to see a collection like this without having to travel miles is worth supporting. Besides, it is amazing just how many visitors have seen the signs on the road for this and other exhibitions they've held here and have then stopped on a whim. I gather the resulting sales have been thoroughly respectable, too.'

Hetty moved round the room slowly. There was only one other visitor, a young man who apparently had already decided to buy a print to give to his girlfriend as a birthday present. (Some present, she was thinking!)

'She'll love it,' the gallery manager was saying, 'and what a good investment.'

The distraction meant that Hetty felt able to stand back and take her time over each print. Modern art was not to her taste, but she found herself exhilarated; impressed by the colour, the perspective and in some cases the texture. It seemed as though she could reach out and run her fingers across rough stone, experience the temperature, smell the fragrance of some of the outrageously brilliant flowers.

Tom allowed her to finish her tour of the room before he said a word. 'Piper only died in 1992. That makes him about as modern as they come. You haven't walked out.'

'I wasn't talking about modern in these terms,' she replied, wishing she had not been quite so didactic about her likes and dislikes.

'Piper was interested in gates and temples of country houses, old buildings that might be bombed out of existence during the Second World War. Do you like 'Clytha Castle'? It was done in 1976. Piper married a Welshwoman, you know. He was persuaded by King George to do twelve views of Windsor Castle. All the king is supposed to have said at the end is, 'You've been pretty unlucky with the weather, Mr Piper.' '

Hetty chortled. 'Fortunately most of what is here is far too big for my wall space.'

'If you had to choose, which would you take?'

There was no hesitation. ' 'Les Junies',' she told him. 'That vivid green is fabulous, even if it is entirely unsuitable for my house.'

'There you go again,' he said, but his exasperation was exaggerated. 'Thinking objectively when all I want you to do is to look at the picture as a work of art. But I'm glad you like the colours. I always knew there was depth to you.'

Hetty was absurdly pleased. 'But I suppose the 'Flowers In A Black Pot' is a better choice.'

'There really is no question of better, or best. It's how you feel a piece works for you. We'll go to Cardiff one day soon. It has the best collection of Post-Impressionists north of Paris.'

Totally at ease with each other, they wandered back to the car. As he helped her into the front seat, Tom bent and kissed her cheek. 'Love the dress,' he said. 'It does something electric to your eyes. That's what I'd like to paint you in. Will you let me, one day?'

She nodded, thinking that, for a mere friend, Tom was remarkably perspicacious. Or had their relationship moved on a fraction? Foolish woman, she chided herself, of course we've moved on. The question is, where?

They found a small restaurant and enjoyed a leisurely lunch. Then Hetty suggested that Tom should take her home.

'I thought we'd go back to Gaer Hill?'

Too fast, far too fast, she thought. 'I really ought to put in an hour or so's reading. I must finish one of the A level texts tonight. And I suppose,' she added gently, 'there are things you have to do to prepare for Megan. Ah, I suppose that also means you won't be at The Grange tomorrow?'

'I'm afraid not,' he said regretfully. 'I have to go to Bristol airport. I have rung Clive so he isn't expecting me.'

'You must put in extra hours next week,' she teased him.

'Not at all. We are volunteers, after all. Sometimes family matters have to come first.'

Hetty sensed she had disappointed Tom. She lifted her chin. Yesterday, last night, had been great: a total surprise, an experience that was as unexpected (at her age) as it had been welcome. If it happened again, that would undoubtedly be excellent. She thought that friendship could stand a lot of that. But not too much and not too soon. There was no way she intended becoming just one of Tom's women.

'Last night was unpredictably delightful,' she said gently, as she stood by her front door to say goodbye to him. 'I had such a lovely day, too. Thank you so much for introducing me to John Piper. I see now that I have missed such a lot by being so hidebound. Please continue nurturing me, Tom. And say nice things to Megan from me. I hope to see you both very soon.'

Hetty stood on her toes to brush his cheek with her lips. As she did so, she had a strong feeling that a curtain twitched.

Balbiro's Journal, 29th July. Later.
From the first I believe I knew exactly what would happen.

Even as we became man and wife, Resham and I, I think I knew it was not meant to be.

Keval tore me from Resham's side. He dragged me from the Gurdwara, through the guests who were looking appalled. I saw Miss Loveridge and Megan shoved to one side. He called me terrible names. I screamed that it was all a mistake, it hadn't happened like that.

Of course I did nothing. I never, in all my life, have done the right thing at the right time. So my father tells me.

Keval thrust me into the back of the waiting car and got in to the driver's seat. We drove home. He pushed me into the house and dragged me upstairs to my bedroom. Then he went outside and locked the door.

All this was without a word except for what he said to me in the Gurdwara.

I wish my mother was here.

Clive was noticeably offhand as he greeted Hetty at The Grange on the Saturday morning, but as Sheila welcomed her enthusiastically saying that now Hetty was there they were sure to finish pegging out the knot garden, Hetty decided it was best to ignore his pursed lips and coolness of manner. She thought they had parted amicably after their last meeting — but with some people resentment lasted for longer than was ever warranted. However, the work the two women did that morning was an excellent job so Clive thawed towards her and, as it became apparent he was meeting Wendy for a drink later, he was all smiles as they left the garden.

Mary Beresford had come over mid-morning with a dish of crabapple jelly and several spoons for them all to try it as she was hoping to add the jelly to her stock of Ottergate produce. It had been decided they would have an open day in the middle of September. While she was there she invited Hetty to supper. This Hetty accepted with pleasure. She would have liked to have seen Tom again but she felt that not only was this unwise quite so soon but that he and Megan needed time alone together to catch up. Supper with Ian and Mary was a most agreeable alternative.

At teatime Megan phoned, so Hetty was able to congratulate her again on her exam success. She also asked how the French holiday had been.

'Sort of cool, I suppose.'

Hetty understood that understatement to mean that it had been a marvellous holiday.

'Do I gather your social life was far from dull?' she teased.

Megan relented. 'It was wicked. There was this other family we got to know and they had French cousins who had wheels so a crowd of us spent quite a lot of time together on the beach and at discos most nights.'

'How did your uncle and aunt feel about that?'

'They were cool. There was a girl of Kate's age so she was happy in the evenings and Pete got off with one of the French girls. Uncle Stephen was just glad he didn't have to ferry us everywhere.'

'And you?'

'I had a great time.' Not for anything would Megan confess that she had resisted attempts to be paired, preferring instead to remain one of the crowd. The earlier events of the summer had jolted her. There was no way she was going to become seriously involved with any boy until she knew him a lot better than was possible during a heady summer holiday. There would be time enough for her, at least, at university.

They did not speak for much longer — for it was apparent that the girl had many friends she wished to contact — but Hetty was able to assure Megan that she was there with any future help that was necessary.

It was as Hetty was leaving for Ottergate that the phone rang again for her. This call was a bolt from the blue, for it was her godmother with the announcement that she was planning a trip to Italy and wanted to come and stay for a night *en route*.

'In an ideal world I hoped you would be able to fetch me from Bristol airport on Tuesday and return me on Thursday for my flight. That will give me a whole day with you. But you must say if it is inconvenient for you to come to the airport and I shall take a taxi.'

'I wouldn't dream of allowing you to do that,' answered Hetty faintly, too astonished even to ask where Dorothy's second flight was heading. 'Just tell me the time you arrive and I'll be there.'

'I should have asked first if you have already made other plans?'

'Not a thing that is as important as seeing you.'

Hetty wrote down the details and put the phone back, her mind reeling. It was not the best of times for a visitor — Hetty still had several hours of work to do for the new school year — but indeed she had nothing planned that was vital. She also had plenty of time to prepare for her guest.

As she was shutting the front door behind her, the phone rang for a third time. Hetty's instinct was to leave the answerphone to pick up the call. Then she wondered if, perhaps, Dorothy had forgotten to mention something urgent and she decided she must take it immediately.

It was not Dorothy, but Tom.

'You didn't ask to speak to me when you spoke to Megan.'

Hetty thought she detected a faint note of accusation. 'No. I didn't know you were there.'

'It never occurred to you.'

'No. Sorry. Was there anything you wanted to tell me, only — '

'You are going out.'

Hetty gazed at the phone in her hand as though it were a weird object. Surely it wasn't as if he had been expecting her to call, was it? Or that Tom thought he had the right to know where she was going? That was not on, for a start. All the same she decided to pander this time to whatever instinct was bugging him. 'I'm having supper with the Beresfords. And I'm a bit late so . . . '

'I won't keep you. I'm glad you're getting

on so well with Mary.'

'She's lovely and we seem to be on each other's wavelength so that I'm quite useful as a sounding board. Ah, Tom, would you be doing anything on Wednesday?'

'As it happens, Wednesday is the one day this week I am totally free. What shall we do?' For the first time he spoke with unguarded warmth.

'It's my godmother. Dorothy Armstrong. You remember, I stayed with her on Mull? Only she is coming here unexpectedly for a couple of nights and I wondered if you would like to come and have a meal?' Hetty stopped, her social impulse draining as rapidly as it had risen. It was extremely unlikely that Tom Gillard would want to socialize with an elderly, unknown woman.

Yet again Tom surprised her by saying that since Hetty had made her godmother sound so formidable a character, he couldn't wait to meet her. They settled on lunchtime.

'Godmother doesn't really care for anything too heavy in the evening so it is better for me to give her a good meal in the middle of the day.'

'I think that will come to all of our digestions in time.' He rang off with a chuckle.

* * *

Ian Beresford cooked for the three of them and after the women had cleared up Mary and Hetty spent a profitable hour or so looking at packaging and labels.

'We have enough for the coming open day but I really need to sort out something better for the future. It's so important to get the visuals right, my business friends tell me. But I'm a firm believer in gut reaction so I decided to obey mine rather than commission a survey.'

'And unnecessarily expensive that would have been, too,' Hetty agreed. 'Pretty but affordable is what you want.'

'Exactly. How fortunate you and I have similar tastes. Shall I top you up?'

'Just half a glass, thank you.'

'So how did you like the Piper exhibition?'

'Very much. How did you know I'd seen it?'

Mary laughed merrily. 'Oh, I have my spies. You'd be surprised.'

'I doubt it,' said Hetty drily. 'I'm becoming used to being the object of local gossip.'

'It is kindly meant, you know. You are a popular teacher so there are an awful lot of people who are concerned about your welfare.'

'My welfare! Do you mean people are anxious about me because now I am living on my own?'

'Something like that. Some of us also worry that you might be scooped up by a gold digger.'

'I thought gold diggers were usually female. Gold diggers!' Hetty spluttered inelegantly over her sip of wine. 'Whatever do you . . . No, you can't mean people are afraid people are after my money . . . '

'Not very clearly put for an English teacher but, yes. Word has it that you have been left fairly well off. Seen any interesting men recently?'

'Mary Beresford. Not you, too?' Hetty was unsure whether to be flattered at a friend's concern or scandalized by the reasoning behind it. 'As it happens, my mother did leave me a little better off than I anticipated but I can assure you it in no way resembles a fortune. Nor, to misquote Jane Austen, am I in need of a husband.'

'Mm. Fine. Fine. We won't speak of it again. Just thought you ought to know. So was it Clive or Tom or Philip who took you to the exhibition?'

'Philip Gerard? You are joking, I hope. Not that I wouldn't be delighted to go to an exhibition with him, you understand, but he

248

does have other fish to fry.'

'I gathered that. I'm glad for him.'

'So am I.'

Hetty hesitated for a moment, hoping she wasn't about to be indiscreet.

'I gather you know about Philip's circumstances.'

'That he has decided to come out? I can't imagine why he left it for so long.'

'Neither can I. But I suppose it does take a lot of courage. He is such a dear, I do hope it is a success for both of them.'

'You mean he kept his love life a secret because he was afraid it might damage his business interests in Otterhaven? Not nowadays, Hetty.'

'You never can tell with a small community.' Hetty was thinking of Laura Blackstone and her cronies. (Would her mother have been censorious? Perhaps that was something better left well alone.) 'There are some people in Otterhaven who will be vile to them, I have no doubt.'

'But not us,' declared Mary. 'Ian and I will have a party for them.'

'That's a splendid idea. I do hope you'll invite me.'

'I shall probably ask you to help with the catering. Joke,' Mary said hastily, as she saw Hetty's look of consternation.

'Have you any idea when Karl takes up residence?'

'Any time now, I should imagine. Philip introduced us only yesterday. The two of them were unloading an old BMW as I was passing.'

Hetty put her head to one side questioningly. 'Nice?'

'Very amiable. Quiet. Looked a bit tired. But I expect that was the stress of the move. Now, tell me more about this visit you made to the Piper exhibition,' said Mary, changing the subject.

Hetty sighed, sensing that Mary would not give up until she had been given at least a morsel of information. 'It was Tom Gillard.'

'How very sensible. I do approve of Tom Gillard. He has character, ability without imposing it on others, kindness and honesty. I'd trust him with a daughter of mine.'

'I'd have thought he was too old for that.' Hetty grinned as she spoke. She was in complete agreement, but not quite inclined to admit it, even to Mary Beresford. 'I wouldn't exactly have called Tom Gillard sensible, though. He's not dull enough for that. But we do have a lot in common. The welfare of his daughter for a start.'

'And quite right, too.'

'I am going home if you continue to tease.'

'Please, don't. It is so refreshing to talk to someone without it being Ottergate, Ottergate — forget I said that — or to do with the pre-teens. Don't forget I said that,' she ended darkly. 'I love the castle and everything I do here and I adore my children but sometimes I get the feeling that nobody sees me as me anymore. Am I making sense?'

'Both sense and nonsense,' said Hetty briskly. 'I'm sure you are as cherished for yourself as ever you would wish. Just think how you would be missed if you were not around,' she added, remembering what Tom had said to her not so long ago about his own wife.

'I suppose you are right'

'Of course I am.'

'Ah, well. Back to the mob,' Mary said, gathering her samples into a neat pile.

'You wait until Jack and Emma are teenagers.'

'When that happens I shall send them to you.'

'Thanks.'

★   ★   ★

The flight from Glasgow to Bristol was on time, Dorothy Armstrong's baggage came off the carousel promptly and they were heading back for South Wales with the modicum of fuss in the shortest possible time. The journey took a little over an hour and their conversation was confined to the scenery, which had not changed, the traffic and the roads, which had, and the state of health of Dorothy's various friends on Mull whom Hetty had met.

'Dear Godmother, you look extremely well,' said Hetty, once she had settled the older woman in the most comfortable chair in the cottage in Otterhaven, a cup of tea at her elbow. 'Almost better than you were when I saw you earlier this summer.'

'Far too many visitors in Scotland this time of year, if you ask me. A peaceful body doesn't want to be bothered with the ravening hordes.'

'So you've decided to join the hordes invading Italy? Why not. But I must say you have given me a surprise — delightful though it is. I can't remember how long it is since you were in Otterhaven.'

'I know. If I had come sooner, I might have seen Joan alive,' Dorothy agreed gruffly.

'I didn't mean . . . You gave up holidays because you said you were much happier at home.'

'That's still the truth.' There was a pause. Hetty passed the digestive biscuits and offered her godmother more tea, which she accepted. 'It's your fault, I think.'

Hetty raised her eyebrows. 'If it is my fault that I am seeing you twice in one summer then I can't be sorry, but I'm not sure I follow your logic.'

'I remember giving you all kinds of extraneous advice while you were staying with me. The old really shouldn't succumb to the temptation of giving the young the benefit of their worldly wisdom. Chances are it isn't wisdom, and it certainly won't be worldly.'

'I think you spoke a lot of sense. Some of it I've already acted on.'

'More fool you. Which part of it was good advice?'

Hetty smiled. 'I guess you'll get to hear about that in due course. But let's get back to you. How exactly are you following your advice to me?'

'It was telling you not to hide yourself away. It was urging you not to let time pass until it was too late. I'm not explaining very well.' For once what Dorothy Armstrong had to say was not in the least concise. It also took time for the whole story to emerge. For what Hetty thought must be the first occasion in Dorothy's life what she had to say actually sounded as though it was being wrung from her.

It had been her own fault, Dorothy confessed, that she had lived all her working life on her own. Hetty already knew that the love of her life had been the man who jilted her. It was for that reason that she had never tried to change jobs once she had achieved the deputy headship. There was always this thought in the back of her mind that one day . . .

'I told you this. Fool that I am, I always thought Alan would want to find me one day.'

'I remember.'

Latterly there had come another man into her life, Dorothy went on to explain. This was a colleague who had recently become a widower. Freed from the constraints of a wife who hated travelling and with a reasonable pension behind him, Donald had embarked on a world cruise. From each port of call he wrote to Dorothy, long letters which she began to look forward to and answered. On his return Donald went back to his small flat on the outskirts of Glasgow, which he had bought when his wife died and where Dorothy visited him regularly, even to the extent of manufacturing the need for a shopping expedition. (This she confessed to Hetty with a defiant air.) In between times they had kept in touch by telephone. Donald had recently taken an apartment in Venice and had invited Dorothy to join him for a week or two.

'He says Scotland is too cold for his aged bones. He says he will probably move on to Malta for the winter. He also says he is missing me.'

'How jolly,' said Hetty warmly. 'You'll have a splendid time in Venice. It's such a beautiful city, and not too large for you to feel overwhelmed — except maybe by the art.'

'If it weren't Venice I doubt if I would contemplate going for one moment,' insisted Dorothy. 'But Venice is a city I've always wanted to visit. There is another thing. It occurred to me, far too late for a woman who thought she knew what she was doing, that if Alan ever came seeking me I might not care to be found by him after all. I had the gall to tell you how to live your life. I realized almost too late that it is high time that I took control of my own destiny. So . . . tell me I'm an old fool and that I should catch the next plane back to where I belong.'

'I shall do no such thing. I think you are doing exactly what you should be doing. I think you have a lot of courage to undertake such an adventure . . . '

'At my age.'

'Age doesn't come into it since you are fit to travel. This is something you want to do.

Go for it! Besides' — Hetty hesitated, then plunged into what she hoped was not discouraging — 'if by some malign chance you found that you were hating every moment of your trip, there is nothing to stop you from coming home immediately.'

Dorothy laughed, albeit shakily. 'I don't think I had got as far as that.'

The clock struck six. Hetty rose. 'Time for a wee whisky, I think.'

It was while she was sipping her whisky — her second — that Dorothy noticed the new painting over the mantelpiece. 'Correct me if I'm wrong, but didn't Joan have an exceedingly lugubrious print of a churchyard in pride of place? I like that one. It's cheerful, yet serene. Of course . . . I even recognize it. Iona. How long have you had it?'

'It was given to me very recently.'

'Ohh. Wait a minute. Didn't you meet an artist while you were staying with me? Don't tell me it's his.'

'There was an artist from Otterhaven staying on Mull. We met quite by chance. He knows how much I like that view.'

Dorothy was on her feet examining the painting minutely. 'He's got the atmosphere of the place. You can feel the softness of the sand, smell the sea. Ah. This artist must like you a lot to paint you into his picture.'

'Not recognizably so. I mean, it's my back view. It could be anyone,' Hetty protested weakly.

'But I recognize the shirt you are wearing. I do like it. The picture, I mean, though the trousers and shirt looked nice enough on you.'

'I hope you'll like the man who painted it. I've invited him for lunch tomorrow. You don't mind, I suppose, Godmother? I thought you might be amused to meet someone different.'

'I look forward to it,' said Dorothy. 'Talking to your gentleman friend will get me into training for entertaining mine.'

★ ★ ★

Hetty and Dorothy settled on a simple cold salmon salad for lunch with new potatoes and some ripe peaches to follow. Hetty arrived in the kitchen to prepare the salad wearing a pair of natural linen trousers and a silk shirt and was dispatched upstairs at once to change into a dress.

'It's an occasion, inviting a gentleman to lunch. You don't want to make him feel unwelcome, do you?'

Hetty did not. She flicked through her wardrobe: too formal, too dull, he'd seen it

257

before . . . In the end and because it was a lovely summer's day, she settled on her new blue. The expression on Dorothy's face made her want to run and change into something that made it appear as though she had made a little less effort — but it was too late. Tom was at the door.

# 13

That day Tom was at his most urbane. He had brought with him a bunch of flowers for Hetty, which impressed Dorothy no end because they were from his own garden instead of a florist: several huge heads of a pale pink lacewing hydrangea and some lavender stalks to give off perfume.

'You'll have to dry all those,' Dorothy said. 'They make wonderful displays in the winter.'

'I know. My mother used to do that every year.'

'Clive Makepeace wants to grow hydrangeas of various varieties at The Grange. You must persuade Mary to add them to her stock,' said Tom.

This entailed a lengthy description of Ottergate's walled garden and Hetty's involvement with it, Dorothy nodding her approbation every minute or so.

Over lunch the conversation turned to Venice. 'I gather this will be your first visit, Miss Armstrong?'

'Tom, please call me Dorothy. There are few cities on this earth that I regret not visiting. Venice was always the first on my list.

I am looking forward to seeing as much as I can in the time available.'

'As much as Donald has the stamina for,' Hetty murmured, which earned her a glare.

'I have already drawn up a list so he knows fine well what he is in for.'

'Then I do hope you have the island of Torcello on your list,' said Tom. 'Apart from the delightful boat ride across the lagoon you will find its cathedral has the most splendid mosaics outside Ravenna. There is a spectacular 'Last Judgement' which I firmly believe rivals the mosaics in St Mark's.'

'Is that so? I do like some of the more macabre subjects. They are very much more satisfying than the mamby-pamby saintly stuff you see in some churches which is supposed to be high art.'

'I do so agree,' said Tom, his face quite straight.

'I doubt it, young man.' But there was a twinkle in Dorothy's eyes. 'I have been admiring the picture of Iona you gave Hetty. That was always one of my favourite views in the days when I cared to make the trip across. Is your work lucrative?'

'Godmother!' Hetty gave a strangled yelp.

Tom did not take offence. 'My local scenes sell very well. As you appreciate, it is important to sell paintings locally unless the

260

view is so well known that it has a wide appeal.'

'Hetty tells me you don't do portraits.'

'No, Dorothy, not as a general rule. Though I did suggest to Hetty that I should paint her.'

'What an excellent idea. I should like to see that.'

'When Hetty wore her blue dress the first time I wanted to paint her then and there.'

'You should paint her in velvet. A deep blue velvet. The richness of the pile would emphasize her skin tones more than this blue, which only offsets her eyes.'

Hetty's face was a study.

'I'd thought of a velvet curtain as a background.'

'Too predictable. Of course, the background is most important. I'd choose something like that stone wall there in the garden. The roughness of the natural material would contrast ideally with the softness of the velvet which invites a caress.'

'I see you have studied art, Dorothy. I'm sure I need not have mentioned anything about Venice you did not already know.'

The two regarded each other with mutual respect.

'The roughness of the stone would undoubtedly emphasize the lines on my face,' said Hetty sourly. 'As for stroking anything — huh!'

'Her mother was the same,' said Dorothy, leaning towards Tom confidentially. 'Joan could never accept a compliment.'

'Hetty has always admired the Pre-Raphaelites, I know that. She is coming to appreciate modern art, too, and that takes application.' He reached over the table and took Hetty's hand, squeezing it briefly and smiling. 'There was a John Piper exhibition only recently and I intend to take her to see a Picasso exhibition soon. Cardiff has a fine collection, too.'

'I've not been to many exhibitions myself recently.'

'Then next time you are in Otterhaven, Dorothy, you must permit me to take you to Cardiff for the day. And I shall begin on Hetty's portrait next week. The blue curtain will do as a cloak and I can sketch the wall as necessary.'

Will she, nill she, Hetty thought as she washed up later, having dispatched Dorothy for a rest on her bed. The nerve of the pair of them. Yet there was no frown on her face, but a significant softening of her lips as she recalled what had been said that lunchtime.

★ ★ ★

Hetty only half-expected Tom to follow up his declared intention of painting her portrait so she was taken aback when he telephoned her at breakfast on Saturday morning to discuss convenient times, settling on a couple of hours every afternoon from the Monday of the following week.

'I've never sat for anyone before. I'm not sure of the procedure.'

'There's nothing to it. You'll see.'

'What do you want me to wear?'

'It doesn't matter, provided the neckline isn't too high. I shall want to drape the velvet curtain myself.'

'You could have saved yourself a phone call and told me later at The Grange.'

'Would you believe it? Meg insists on a shopping expedition and an exploratory tour of the campus. I don't expect there is a thing we can do about going into the halls of residence on a Saturday, but you know Meg. I think I shall insist on getting something out of it for myself and doing a concert or whatever is available. She still hasn't seen the inside of the Millennium Centre, either.'

'It sounds as though you are going to have a busy weekend.'

'It will be the weekend.' He sounded regretful. 'I've some old friends coming for lunch on Sunday.'

And naturally their relationship, such as it was, did not merit inclusion in a reunion with old friends. What was she expecting? 'Of course you're going to be busy. See you on Monday then, Tom.'

Hetty and Sheila spent the morning double-digging the trench for the box plants in the knot garden, infilling with well-rotted compost. It was hard work and by the end of it Hetty was exhausted, so much so that she was very glad Tom was not starting her portrait that afternoon, for she was sure the tiredness was all too evident on her face.

Afterwards she had a suspicion that it was because of this tiredness she was unaware of Clive's duplicity. As she was getting into her car — the last to leave except for him — Clive came half-running over to her.

'Nearly missed you,' he exclaimed, 'and then you would have been very fed up with me. We've decided to meet for a drink this evening and discuss our future plans in a civilized atmosphere.' He named a nearby pub. 'You will be there, won't you? I do hope you don't have anything else planned. I don't want anyone to be left out.'

Hetty sighed inwardly. There were more congenial ways she could think of in which to spend her Saturday evening. It was just unfortunate they were not on offer. On the

264

other hand, she would be feeling more rested and therefore more capable of adding something to the discussion.

'That'll be fine, Clive. Thanks for including me. I'll see you later.'

★ ★ ★

It was not an evening for either the spotted linen or the blue, she decided. Remembering that Sheila at least was more likely to be wearing serviceable trousers, Hetty chose the natural linen ones which had so offended Dorothy, a T-shirt and a smart/casual jacket.

Clive's car was in the car park but Hetty realized she could not recall what either Wendy or Sheila drove. She might even be the first to arrive. She shrugged. Then she stopped. It was a little odd that Clive had been so insistent that she came when he must have known that Tom could not that evening. Tom's input must be of more value than her own since he had been in on the project from the start.

With a growing sense of unease, Hetty entered the pub. Clive was on his own in a corner. He rose to greet her, kissing her cheek as he sat her down beside him on a sofa. 'You'll never believe it,' he said. 'First Sheila phoned to say she had an unexpected visitor.

Then Wendy phoned to say she had developed a headache and as she drives Jane neither of them would be able to come. So I'm afraid it looks as though it's just the two of us,' he said, looking anything but sorry. 'I do hope you don't mind. What do you say to making an evening of it and having a meal? And to start with, what are you drinking?'

'I thought it was going to be a short evening,' she protested, becoming more furious as Clive Makepeace spoke. 'I did tell you that I am very busy. I have a text to finish this evening. You promised we wouldn't be long.' She was now absolutely certain that he had set her up — but short of making a scene in public and walking out there was very little she could do about it.

'Well,' he said, 'you know how it is when several people start discussing something that is dear to their hearts. I had a vague feeling all along that we might be here for the duration, but there it is. What is their loss is very much my gain.'

'If it is such an important meeting,' she persisted crossly, 'I'm a little surprised that neither Ian nor Mary is here, not to mention Tom.'

'They were all busy this evening. Besides,' he went on smoothly, 'Ian leaves most of this sort of thing to me. He relies on my expertise to suggest plans that will work.'

'Which I am sure you do,' she said. 'You were offering me a drink?'

'Presumably you were eating at home so why don't we have something here as well as that drink?'

He was right; Hetty had intended making herself an omelette. She did have to eat though, she thought resignedly, and she might as well do so immediately so she settled on a portion of chicken-in-a-basket and a soft drink, reasoning that they would arrive speedily and she could get away the sooner. Yet in spite of the inauspicious beginning, the time passed amicably.

Clive Makepeace certainly knew his subject and once she had steered the conversation to walled gardens, he waxed lyrical on grand designs of the past. 'It is a shame we can't contemplate anything quite like that,' he ended, 'but you never know what might happen in the future.'

'Mary Beresford certainly has excellent plans for the castle,' Hetty said. 'But I imagine you have heard most of them from her already.'

'She is talking nonsense about packaging and so on. I mean, what's wrong with a plain white recycled paper bag?'

Hetty latched on to the recycled angle,

determined not to become involved in anything more contentious. 'You must mention that to her yourself,' she urged him. 'I'm sure they can be sourced easily enough. Now, I really must go. August seems to gallop, don't you find? And my schedule was disrupted by an unexpected visit from an elderly godmother.'

'I'm sure you made her feel most welcome. Is she very aged?'

'The same age as my mother would have been.' To her relief and a little to her surprise, the information emerged without the grief Hetty had experienced all too frequently.

'Not too energetic a lady, then.'

'On the contrary, my godmother was merely visiting me *en route* to Venice, where she has been invited to stay by a friend.'

'I cannot for the life of me understand this pressing need so many people have nowadays to dash all over the world on a mere whim. Think of the pollution, the global warming. Still, I suppose your godmother can hardly be said to be one of life's gallivanters at her age.'

Hetty gritted her teeth. Not for the world would she admit that gallivanting was precisely what Dorothy Armstrong was doing at that very moment. 'I suppose that means you rarely go abroad yourself?'

'No, indeed I do not. I cannot abide food

messed around the way foreigners prepare it and as for the smells . . . Don't tell me you enjoy foreign travel, Hetty.'

'Of course I do. Or I would if I had the opportunity. Once I retire I most certainly intend to rectify that.' Hetty got to her feet resolutely. 'I really must go now, Clive.' She made her way determinedly to the bar, where the bill was presented. She already had a note in her hand and so Clive was forced to permit her to share their costs.

In the car park he held her car door for her but before she could slide in behind the wheel he caught hold of her. His kiss was clumsy (one could forgive lack of practice), uninvited and definitely unwelcome (and that was not forgivable).

'Please don't do that again, Clive,' she said coldly, when she was able.

'But women like to be kissed, don't they? Particularly women of . . . How do they put it? Women of a certain age like to feel that their youth has not utterly disappeared. It gives them a sense of agelessness. I mean, without a man of your own you must be very lonely — '

'Stop this at once.'

'But I have seen you. First of all it was that bookseller. You didn't know he was a homo, did you? Then it was Tom Gillard. I saw you

269

with him the other day. Amazing. After all, no one can call a woman of your age a spring chicken, can they?'

'How dare you speak to me like that.'

It seemed that he was not used to his actions being challenged. Like a deflated balloon Clive Makepeace's arrogance dissolved almost as quickly as it had reared its head. 'I-I didn't mean . . . '

It was the gall of it. It was not the hang-dog expression on his face; it was the conceited assumption that she was so sex-starved that she could not wait to be mauled that so infuriated Hetty. 'But I do mean it, Clive. I do not welcome your . . . attentions. I am not lonely.' She paused and her voice altered to cold anger. 'You set me up tonight. I don't believe either Wendy or Sheila were even invited — although I'll spare your embarrassment by not asking them outright. But if you want me to continue working at The Grange, nothing like this must ever, ever happen again. I do hope I have made myself quite clear.'

It was the schoolmistress in her that enabled Hetty to sound so icily enraged that finally penetrated Clive's consciousness. Stunned, he shook his head as if only then did he understand just what he had done to deserve her ire. His stuttering apology almost made her smile as she drove off, though in reality Hetty was appalled. It had been outrageous. She had not encouraged Clive in any way. She thought back to the occasions when she had been alone in his company — and those when others had been present. She could not imagine what in her behaviour had induced him to believe that she had any interest in him other than as a colleague.

Damn the man. She really was enjoying the work with Sheila in the knot garden. Perhaps if they were to finish what they were doing she might enlist Sheila's help to ensure that Clive left her strictly alone? It bore thinking about.

★   ★   ★

Tom Gillard arrived promptly on Monday afternoon. After careful consideration Hetty had decided on the natural linen trousers and a beige T-shirt, reasoning that the colour would not stand out against blue velvet. She had also swept the ground in front of the stone wall and tidied a few of her pots in case he wanted to use any of those in the background.

He greeted her coolly. She was a little taken aback, given the degree of intimacy that had gone before, but she decided that this was, after all, his professional work and so anything more might be considered a distraction.

'Do you want me to use a chair or a stool?' she asked, indicating her garden seats.

'Would we be able to move that stone seat?' he asked, pointing to a slab of stone partly hidden by a wisteria that had not yet been cut back.

'Not without a crane, I should imagine.'

He did not respond to her attempt at humour. 'I've brought a camera,' he said. 'I'd like to take close-ups of the wall, and I'll take the stone seat also. Today you can sit on an ordinary chair and I'll paint in the stone later.'

'Oooh, cheating.' She smiled.

Again he did not return her smile. Without a word he placed one of her garden chairs in front of the wall and gestured for her to sit on it. Hetty shrugged her shoulders and complied. Tom produced the velvet curtain and with totally impersonal hands and an impassive face draped it round her, manipulating the fabric skilfully so that it began to resemble a gown.

'You've done this before,' Hetty murmured. His face was close to hers but any suggestion that their lips might meet was obviously out of the question. The aura of indifference seemed impenetrable.

'As Dorothy said, you have to learn about the nature of fabric, any sort of fabric — what it will do, and what is unnatural, its texture and so on. That's part of my job.'

'So what happens this afternoon?' she asked, as evenly as she might, making the decision that to be offended at what was a put-down could still be construed as overreacting.

'As I said, I'll take photographs. Of you in various poses, of the surroundings, close-ups of things that I might use. Then I'll go home and put something on to canvas.'

'It doesn't sound as though you need me at all.'

'On reflection I think that is right.'

Hetty swallowed a lump in her throat, unable to think what to say next. There was an edge to Tom's voice that was unmistakable; the whole atmosphere was badly wrong.

'Of course, I shall need you to pose for me when I actually paint your face but the bulk of everything else I can do from a photo.'

'How different from the artists who painted in Parisian garrets,' she managed.

Tom made no response.

This was altogether too much. 'What's the matter, Tom?' Hetty asked desperately.

'Is it Megan? Has she had bad news? It's not Balbiro, is it?'

'There is nothing the matter.'

'Come off it. You've been uncommunicative ever since you arrived. Normally I can't get a word in edgeways.' He did not even rise to this. Hetty went on despondently, 'I can't imagine what, but something has happened. Won't you tell me? Please.'

Tom, who had been focusing his digital camera and recording what was most appropriate, paused. 'I had thought that after the night we spent together you might have managed to keep your hands off Clive Makepeace.'

Hetty's jaw literally dropped.

'I see you don't deny it. Well, there it is. I said I'd paint your portrait and as I might develop portraiture that is what I shall do. And, thanks to modern technology, the actual number of times I need you to pose for me can be kept to the minimum. But I don't think there is any necessity for us to pretend there is any sort of a relationship between us, do you?'

'And I don't suppose you would be open to any sort of an explanation, given that you have come to the conclusion that most appeals to you. Is this going to take much longer, or have you finished?'

'I've quite finished,' he replied tightly. 'I'll be in touch when I need to come again. Keep the velvet. It'll save me from remembering to bring it. No, don't bother to let me out. I can do that myself.'

The next moment Hetty heard the front door close. The sound came with a finality that dismayed her.

Men, thought Hetty. Thank heavens I teach only girls. What it must be like to have half a class of teenage boys with raging testosterone, I cannot imagine.

Was that what it was? Was Tom Gillard really jealous of Clive Makepeace? What had he been talking about? Ah, she thought, of course. It was obviously that scene in the car park But how? Why? Tom had said hurtful things. Maybe he had not been quite so cutting as Clive but he had been unkind. If he imagined she was going to beg and plead and justify herself, demean herself in order that he would forgive her. Forgive me! Huh. Fat chance I'll be forgiving him in a hurry.

Then it occurred to Hetty with startling clarity that what was happening to her now was in no small way what must have happened to Balbiro. Both she and the Sikh girl had been caught in compromising situations. No matter that there was no truth in the accusations, no matter that their ages were a generation apart, that the mores of their cultures were different, they had been judged by the men who controlled — wanted, expected to control — them, and been found guilty.

It was beyond doubt an appalling thought.

Hetty's righteous indignation evaporated. She burst into tears.

The tears lasted for some time. They were painful, gut-wrenching sobs that shook her whole frame, far worse than when she had first grieved for her mother. After a while she realized that the sun had gone in and the velvet cloth, which had slipped to the ground in her misery, was no longer protecting her from a cold breeze which had sprung up. She was shivering violently. She got up with difficulty, all her joints stiff and aching.

Hetty had just picked up a warm cardigan, which was lying across the sofa, when the doorbell rang. Oh hell, she thought immediately. She knew she must look a complete mess. She thought wildly that she'd not answer it. There was no one she was expecting. Or was it Tom, come back to apologize? Hetty ran to the door and flung it open.

'Tom . . . ' she said, and stopped.

'Hi,' said Mary Beresford. 'I waited, because I knew Tom was coming this afternoon and that you would be in. Oh my God.' She clapped her hand to her forehead. 'I've committed the sin of tactlessness. He's still . . . ' Her voice dropped exaggeratedly. 'Here. Not . . . ' She got no further.

Tears were rolling down Hetty's face.

'May I?' Mary pushed Hetty gently back inside the house and closed the front door behind them without waiting for assent. 'I guess you won't want the whole street to see you in this state. Come into the kitchen and sit down. Here, put on this cardi you seem to have dropped. Now, what you need is a cup of tea.'

'Wh-what I need is a stiff drink,' Hetty snivelled, huddling into the cardigan.

'Tea first. For shock. After that we'll go for the alcohol.' Mary had put on the kettle and found the box of tissues which were next to the kitchen radio. She handed Hetty a large handful of them. 'Blow your nose and wipe your eyes,' she said, as though Hetty was one of her little ones. 'I think a good strong Assam is what is required right now. With plenty of sugar.'

'I d-don't take sugar.'

'You do today.' Mary placed a mug of tea on the table in front of Hetty. 'Drink up. As hot as you can take it. That's better,' she said with satisfaction as she saw some colour return to her friend's face. 'Now,' she said, 'is there anything you feel you can tell me? Not that I'm prying,' she added, 'but there may be something I can do to help. What's happened?'

Hetty told her. She omitted nothing. Afterwards Hetty could not remember ever having been so frank with a woman friend. There were things she had told Dorothy. (There were things she had told Tom, and wished she hadn't.) She had confided in her mother on only the most mundane of subjects. And she had never been able to open herself in this way to a woman friend. She did not regret it on this occasion.

To Hetty's surprise Mary did not condemn Tom outright — though she laughed about Clive Makepeace. 'I guess you handled Clive in just the right way,' she commented. 'As for Tom, well, the man is a fool, but a fool in love is forgivable.'

'In love? Come off it. He hates me.'

'I'm not going to say hate is akin to love . . . Well, I guess I just did. You know what I mean. When he knows the truth he'll come begging for forgiveness. You wait and see.'

'But I am not going to beg,' said Hetty

stubbornly. 'I'm not even going to attempt to explain what happened.'

'So it's an impasse? Uh-oh, why is it otherwise sensible adults insist on acting like small children when their feelings are bruised?'

'I don't know.' Hetty smiled tremulously. 'Suppose you tell me.'

'I just might. Though I think a large glass of red wine might aid the process. Got anything in the house?'

'Didn't you drive in?' But Hetty got up and fetched a bottle of Shiraz, a corkscrew and two glasses.

'Ian dropped me off. He has a meeting which is likely to go on for a good hour or more. Enough time to finish this between us, anyway. Don't worry, I'll keep Ian away from you. You probably won't want to see any man for the next twelve hours or so, though rage has made your eyes sparkle. I'm amazed Tom didn't rush you straight to bed from sheer abandoned ardour.'

'I might have been seething with wrath but I'm glad to say I was totally unapproachable. That's the teacher in me. And now my eyes are merely red-rimmed. I shall go to bed when we've finished the bottle. I don't even think I could face *Animal Farm* tonight.'

'An excellent idea. You'll feel so much better in the morning.'

Bilbaro's Journal, 29th July. Later still.
I do not know what will happen next. Or maybe I do.
Scenario 1:
Keval will bring my husband back to the house and insist that we talk together. (My husband. I like the sound of that. I wish . . . How I wish that I could call Resham my husband for the rest of our lives.) As for Keval, well, whatever he still suspects, it is in our family's interests that we sort this matter out so that our reputations are not entirely ruined. It affects his reputation, too. Why did I never think of that? When the time comes for Keval to marry, no other family will want him if they think shame has befallen us. Our father always said that as soon as I am married they will begin to look for a suitable bride for Keval.
I'm not sure what he thinks about that.
I have not understood my brother for a long time.
But if he brings Resham here, all will be well.
Scenario 2:
Keval will punish me for all the ills he believes I have brought down on us.
This has always been my fate.
I don't know how much time I have left to finish this journal which I will put in a bag and tie round

my waist. If I do not survive, maybe one day the truth will be known.

He comes.

I can hear only one set of footsteps.

# 14

In the morning there was food shopping to do. Returning home with her hands full of heavy plastic bags, the handles of which cut into her, Hetty wondered not for the first time if the moment had come for her to haul out her mother's old shopping trolley, which she had scorned for as long as she could recall. The trolley might be hideous — and a danger to other pavement users — but it was practical.

As Hetty passed Philip Gerard's bookshop the bookseller emerged, followed by another man.

'Hetty!' Philip exclaimed. 'Serendipitous encounter. Come and meet Karl.'

Hetty put down her bags and shook Karl's hand while the formal introductions were made.

'Welcome to Otterhaven,' she said warmly. 'I do hope you'll like living among us.'

'I'm sure he will,' said Philip exuberantly, so that there was no mistaking his pleasure. 'I can't think why it took us this long to do the obvious.'

Karl merely smiled. He was a little older

than Philip, Hetty judged, his face drawn, the skin round his eyes etched with fine lines, and his lips were pale but his expression as he looked at Philip revealed a great deal more than friendship.

'I have to get my shopping home,' Hetty said. 'But I do hope I'll see you again soon. You must both come for a meal.' She admired the courage of the two men who had decided to live their lives the way they believed was best for them. She did so hope it would work out.

She had just turned the corner when she almost bumped into Megan. This was a meeting that could have been fraught with awkwardness. Both faces reflected it. It was Megan who saved the day, clumsily embracing Hetty, bags and all. The embrace said eloquently that whatever Megan did or did not know about the relationship between her father and Hetty, at least she was aware that there had been a quarrel.

'I don't know about you and Dad,' the girl said, her voice choked with tender emotion. 'I despair of the two of you.'

Hetty put down her bags carefully, her eyes filling. She fumbled for the tissue in the pocket of her jacket to blow her nose.

'Sorry,' she said. 'I despair of me, too.'

'I don't really want to hear the details,'

Megan went on. 'I do think you might want to know that Dad has decided he simply has to go to Pembrokeshire to do some seascapes. Apparently there are fantastic sightings of dolphins this year and he says he can't afford to miss the opportunity.'

'No, I suppose not,' agreed Hetty, who could appreciate the call of work. She hesitated. 'How long will he be away?'

'Who knows?' The girl shrugged her shoulders. 'Just as long as it takes him to calm down. Whatever did you say to him?' she said, curiosity getting the better of her. 'I can't ever remember Dad getting quite so het up over a girlfriend. Er . . . sorry. I probably shouldn't have mentioned girlfriends. Not that they were much in evidence. I mean, there wasn't one who really mattered . . . '

'It's all right, Megan,' said Hetty, managing an even tone and a smile that was in fact doleful. 'There's no need to explain. It was all a silly misunderstanding. If Tom — your father wants an explanation, he'll ask for it, I expect.'

'And if he decides to be stubborn you won't bother to enlighten him,' Megan said shrewdly.

This time Hetty's smile was genuine. 'You sound just like Mary Beresford,' she exclaimed. 'Very adult. Much more adult than I am. But tell me,' she continued, thinking that the conversation had dwelt for far too long on her absurd affairs, 'if your father has gone away for a few days, does that mean you have had your place at Cardiff confirmed?'

'The letter came just when you said it would, and also the offer for a hall of residence. I sent the forms back straight away.'

'That's good. Where will you be going?'

'It looks like I've managed to get what I wanted,' said Megan, with a grin. 'At first Dad was adamant about me going to an all-female hall, but eventually we compromised when I agreed to one which offers an evening meal.'

They discussed Megan's choice, which Hetty said she thought was sensible. 'Though I have a feeling you might be one of those who could manage to cater for herself,' she added. 'Anyway, once you have acquired a group of friends you can always look for somewhere to share together next year.'

'That's what Dad said. Hetty, do you think you might come shopping with me this week?'

'Of course I will,' said Hetty readily. 'But I thought you went shopping with your father the other day.'

'It was a disaster,' said Megan darkly. 'He hasn't a clue.'

Hetty chuckled, thinking that poor Tom must have been beset by the tastes of his teenaged daughter. 'I suppose you have a budget?'

'He gave me a cheque yesterday when he decided to go to Pembrokeshire. Said he washed his hands of me. We didn't quite come to blows about it. Oh, I didn't mean that Dad rows frequently. He's not that sort of a man at all. I mean — '

'I know, Megan. And I'm very flattered you think I might be able to help. When shall we go, and where would you prefer to shop?' They settled on the following day and Cribbs Causeway.

'It's even got a Karen Millen.'

'If your budget runs to that,' said Hetty, her eyebrows raising, 'though I guess the sales might still be on. Megan,' she continued in a rush as the girl turned to go, 'is there any more news of Balbiro? I passed on what I knew — which was little enough — to Tom, but I've heard nothing more recent than a couple of weeks ago. Surely someone has heard something by now. And what about Keval? Has there been any news about him?'

'I'm going to see Jit this afternoon as it happens. I guess I'll find out then.'

'You've obviously heard that her place at Cardiff is also secure.'

'Isn't it great? I can't believe she finally persuaded her family to agree to let her go. Anyway, I am sure to hear the latest news of Balbiro, whatever that is. Would you like to come with me?'

Hetty was about to agree, then she thought better of it. 'Thank you, but you enjoy yourselves alone. In fact, I'm a little surprised you aren't doing your shopping with Jit. She's your age and will have your tastes.'

'Not really. If she hadn't married I suppose she might have chosen to wear a few fashionable things, but I get the impression that if Sobha doesn't approve, Jit does as he wants.'

Hetty did so hope this form of control would not extend to Jit's activities at university. Then she thought that Sobha might just be controlled by his wife sufficiently for her to manage her life to her own satisfaction.

'I'll see you tomorrow.'

★ ★ ★

Their shopping expedition was cancelled. During the evening while Hetty was sitting reading, Megan phoned. 'Hetty . . . It's

287

Balbiro. It's blowing my mind. Jit's family . . . I've only just got home. I had to wait ages for a taxi. The bus was cancelled. Oh, Hetty . . . '

'What's happened?' The girl sounded hysterical. 'Are you all right?' This was quite unlike the Megan she had come to know and love. 'Did you say Jit's family is in a state? Tell me?'

There was a sob down the phone. 'Balbiro has been found but . . . '

The sobs were getting louder. 'Is your father still away?'

'Y-yes.'

'I'm coming over right now. Make yourself a strong cup of tea and keep warm. Best for shock. I won't be long. You can tell me everything when I get there.'

Hetty grabbed a thick cardigan and her car keys. She drove as fast as she thought was safe through the narrow lanes — though once it was necessary to use car lights in the evening at least you could see on-coming traffic through the hedges. Megan hadn't made sense, she was thinking. But there was only one possible explanation for the Singhs to be in a state if Balbiro had been found, and she shivered.

Megan was sitting at the kitchen table, hunched over herself as though she was in pain. She was wearing only a thin T-shirt and she had made no attempt to put the kettle on. Hetty gave her a brief hug and put her own cardigan round the girl's shoulders. Then she filled the kettle.

'Tell me again,' she said calmly. 'Did you say 'found', Megan? That Balbiro has been found? Surely that's good news?'

'Balbiro is dead.'

She had feared that. Hetty sat down next to Megan and took her freezing hands in her own warm ones. 'When was she found?'

'This morning.'

What dreadful timing for Megan to appear at their house when Manjit and Balbir had only just found out what had happened to their niece.

'Where was Balbiro found?'

'In the attic at her home. It's doing my head in. She was stuffed into a trunk. Keval killed her.'

It was too much to take in. Hetty felt quite helpless. She couldn't cope with anything so horrendous as this on her own. Megan's father should be here to support her.

'Where is your father staying?'

'I've forgotten.'

'Surely he must have left a phone number?'

'Oh. Yes. I suppose it's in the usual place,' Megan said vaguely.

'And that is . . . '

'We always leave our contact numbers by the phone in the hall.'

It was a mobile number. Hetty punched in the digits, praying that there would be a signal; that Tom had left his mobile on. When he answered after only a few rings — of course, he was expecting it to be his daughter at the other end — she spoke briskly.

'Megan is all right, Tom, but she's in a bit of a state. If it is possible, I think you should come home immediately.'

'Hetty? Where are you? Where's Meg? What's happened?'

Hetty explained crisply, not wanting to dwell on the dreadfulness of the death or on speculations as to the how and the why of it. 'Please come home, Tom. She needs you.'

It would take him a little more than two hours, Tom judged. He could leave immediately, once he had settled his bill and thrown his things into his car. 'The traffic should be reasonable at this hour.'

'I'll stay here until you arrive.'

The white-faced Megan was still huddled at the kitchen table. Despite Hetty's cardigan she was trembling. Hetty switched the kettle on again and found teabags and mugs.

'Would you like to go to bed?' she asked gently, handing Megan a mug of sweetened tea. 'You could have your tea there. Would you have such a thing as a hot water bottle? You'd probably warm up more quickly.'

Megan shook her head mutely.

'Then why don't I light a fire in the sitting-room?' suggested Hetty. The kitchen only had hard chairs and as there was no heating on, it wasn't too warm, either. Nor could she see immediately how to switch on the cottage's heating. But she knew that a wood fire was already laid in the fireplace. In the hearth was a box of matches and she struck a match, hoping the fire would catch straight away, which it did as the wood was dry. Once it was going well, Hetty put the guard in front of it while she fetched the duvet and a pillow from Megan's bed, along with a towelling robe, which was hanging on her bedroom door. Then she coaxed the girl on to the wide couch, pulling off her trainers, putting on her dressing gown (clumsily, because she had no experience of this sort of thing, she thought whimsically) and covering her snugly with the duvet.

After that Hetty put on her own cardigan again and made herself comfortable in a chair near Megan, noticing with relief that with the tea inside her the girl's eyelids were becoming heavy.

'Have a little sleep,' she said softly. 'Your

father will be here when you wake,' trusting that it would be so. 'You can tell us what happened together. Go to sleep, Megan.'

Just before midnight Hetty, whose own eyes had been closing intermittently, saw the lights of Tom's car sweep into the drive, heard the final rev of the engine, the sound of the car door slamming shut. Awake in an instant, she was in the hall as his key opened the door.

Oddly it had not occurred to her to wonder how they would greet each other after the awkwardness of their last meeting. Her presence had come about because his daughter had been desperate for an adult's support and she, Hetty, had been the only one within reach whom Megan felt she could trust. Suddenly she was very unsure how Tom, who'd had over two hours to reflect, would interpret this. She feared he might well think it unwarranted interference.

But there was not the slightest hesitation on Tom's part. Leaving the door wide open he strode into the hall and took Hetty into his arms, hugging her to him, pressing her face into his shoulder, his hand gently stroking her head.

'Thank God you were here for her,' he said simply, after a moment. 'Thank you so much for coming over. Not on my account, but hers. I could have no right to ask you for anything. I think, maybe, I made more than a fool of myself the other day . . . '

Hetty had slowly manoeuvred herself free. Now she put a soft finger against his mouth. 'It doesn't matter. Shut the door and come into the kitchen. Megan's asleep on the couch and I think she's better not woken too abruptly.'

'What on earth has happened? Are we talking murder, for God's sake?'

'I don't know. I decided it would be better for Megan only to have to tell us once. She's obviously in shock but at least she knows she's warm and safe and that you will be here when she wakes.'

'I suppose it's an honour killing. Honour . . . I need a drink,' he said, going to the cupboard. 'A stiff whisky. What about you?'

'That sounds great. Have you eaten? I had earlier, just before Megan phoned me, but you might not have had time.'

'I had just finished eating when you called, thanks. I might get some bread and cheese, though.'

They took the whisky and the bread and cheese and went through into the sitting-room to find Megan fully awake and sitting up.

'You needn't have come home, Dad. Hetty

shouldn't have worried you.'

'On the contrary, I am very glad she did.' He bent down to kiss the top of her head. 'Poor kitten, you've had a hell of a shock, by the sound of it, and shouldn't have to bear it on your own.'

'Balbiro did.'

Hetty fetched tissues, for herself and Megan.

'Do you want to tell us?' Tom asked, when Megan had finished blowing her nose and wiping her eyes.

'Sorry. I'm ready now.' She took a deep breath to steady herself. 'Do you remember I told you Keval had gone back to India? All this is because of him, of course.'

'Why don't you start at the beginning?'

At first Megan thought she couldn't possibly put any of it, the dreadfulness of it, into words, but as she began to tell her father and Hetty what she had discovered that afternoon she found that marshalling her thoughts became easier.

'They, the Singhs, said that Keval was increasingly alienated from his friends over the last few months. Well, I knew that because Jit had mentioned it and it was obvious that Balbiro was wary of his attitude. He didn't like the British way of life, saying it had been forced on him.'

Keval and Balbiro had been taken back to Punjab a couple of years previously to visit relatives, but whereas, like her cousin, Balbiro hated the experience, Keval had found there something that was lacking in his own life. He saw and admired a vibrancy where his sister could not see beyond the squalor.

'I think I understand how it was with him,' said Megan. 'So when the family returned he became more and more restless. His parents did suggest that they should find him a wife — though I can't see what good that would have done.'

Hetty and Tom exchanged enigmatic glances.

'Anyway, it was agreed that they would marry off Balbiro first. I think Keval wasn't too happy about their choice for her but Resham's family was all for it. Then, because there was this stupid lack of communication between them all, Balbiro got it into her head that all Resham wanted was a marriage of convenience and she ran away.'

'To you.'

'Yes, Dad. It was all my fault. I know that.'

'On the contrary,' said Hetty firmly, 'it would have been far, far worse if she had gone to Birmingham or some other large city instead, which I gather is what she originally intended. I doubt if her family would have forgiven her then. It was just unlucky that your brother turned up when he did.'

'That's the whole point,' said Megan. 'It was another piece of idiocy on Keval's part. He just worried away at the whole event and naturally in the end Balbiro confessed.'

'To what? To meeting a young man in the house of her friend?'

'It was enough. Balbiro was beaten by her father but when her mother insisted that she was still a virgin Keval agreed reluctantly not to try to prevent the marriage.'

'How do you know all this?' Hetty interrupted, thinking that Jit must have been extremely frank with her friend.

'Balbiro was locked in her room. She had been keeping a journal and once all the trouble started after the weddings, to keep it safe she strapped the book under her trousers. When she was found . . . in the attic . . . in the trunk . . . I can't say it,' she broke off abruptly. 'It's like, surreal . . . '

'Dear, you don't have to go on,' said her father.

'Yes, I do,' she said fiercely. 'Balbiro's parents found the journal on her. They read it and told everyone.'

'But it must have been clear from the journal that nothing happened here that was truly detrimental to Balbiro's reputation,'

Hetty persisted. 'So why did it all go so terribly wrong for her?'

'I don't know, I think Keval may have let slip something to one of his closer friends. Anyway, gossip started . . . And you know the rest because you were there.'

'I only know what happened at the weddings.'

'Keval dragged Balbiro home. We saw that. Then he beat her. Though he did kill her accidentally. He said she fell and hit her head on the corner of a chest of drawers. He didn't tell anyone but concealed her . . . her body in the attic.'

Tears were streaming down her face. Tom went over to sit beside her, gently mopping her face with more tissues. Then he cuddled her to himself. There was a pause while Megan grew calmer.

'I still don't see how you know that part in such detail,' Hetty prompted gently.

'Keval took himself off to relatives in Punjab. Once he was there . . . I don't really understand it . . . But he seems to have got a conscience or something. Anyway, he wrote to his family. He told them it was an accident, that she fell and hit her head. He said it was obviously meant for her to die because it was a matter of honour.'

'Honour . . . ' said Hetty scornfully,

echoing Tom's words.

'It must have been just awful. That's what I can't get my head around. That he could have ... That he could ... in the attic. So her father found her in a trunk. They had to call the police.'

'What will happen now?'

'Who knows?' said Tom. 'Investigations. A manslaughter charge? All very complicated, anyway. Whether Keval is brought back and faces justice is anyone's guess.'

'It'll take years,' said Hetty prophetically.

'Jit's mother says Resham is distraught. He blames himself for not going after them when Keval dragged Balbiro away. He keeps saying he should be rescuing her on a white charger. Weird. Do you imagine it's a reference to the white horse the bridegroom always rides on to his wedding in Bollywood films?'

'It is his fault, in a way,' said Tom, raising his eyebrows, for he was not a Bollywood fan. 'Resham ought to have told Balbiro his true feelings in the first place.'

'And now he is threatening to find Keval and kill him.'

'And so it will go on,' said Tom sombrely. 'Meg, love. Let's get you to bed. You need sleep.'

'Sleep . . . '

'It's desperately sad but try not to think

about it too much. Oh, how banal. But try not to dwell on it, at least, not tonight. Perhaps tomorrow you could call Jit? She must be feeling even worse than you are,' suggested Hetty, earning herself a glance of gratitude from Tom.

Together they persuaded Megan to go to bed, fussing over her gently until she seemed inclined to sleep.

'Though whether she will is very doubtful,' said Tom, as they returned downstairs to the fire. He threw on another log and helped himself to another whisky, first offering to refill Hetty's glass.

'The young are surprisingly resilient,' said Hetty, declining the top-up. 'And now, I guess I'd better get myself home. Just look at the time.'

'Don't go. We have a few things to clear up ourselves, don't we?'

'Wouldn't it be better to leave it until tomorrow?' suggested Hetty, who feared one or other of them would say something regrettable at that late hour and after the trauma of Megan's revelations.

'No,' said Tom stubbornly. 'I need you to know that I have had time to think while I was away and that I'm well aware I'm all sorts of a fool, also that I'm prepared to talk about it.'

Hetty sat down again on the couch. 'If you are talking about what you think happened with Clive, then yes, you are,' she agreed.

'Why don't you tell me what really happened. On second thoughts,' said Tom hastily, 'I have no right to ask you to do anything of the sort.' He sat on the couch with her, but at the far end of it.

Hetty's eyes narrowed. 'Oh, you are a devious man, Tom Gillard,' she hissed softly. 'Telling me I don't have to is a way of making sure that I will.' Control, she was thinking. Why was it that men had to control?

'My God, do you have such a bad opinion of me?'

'Of course not, and I don't intend to quarrel with you, either. If you must know, Clive got me to the pub on false pretences — said that the rest of the team was coming too. To cut a long story short, we had something to eat, then I said I was going. He pounced in the car park. As you saw.'

'The rat. I'll knock his teeth in.'

Hetty sighed audibly. 'No, you won't. I've dealt with Clive and that's an end to it.'

'Does that mean you'll be giving up the garden?'

'Certainly not.'

'Ah. Hetty . . . ' He was turning his glass round and round in his fingers, his eyes fixed on the contents.

'You'll spill that.' She leant across and took the glass from him. Then she kissed him. 'Is that better?' she said when she drew back. Not far enough.

It was some minutes before either drew breath.

'Does this mean we are an item, as the young call it?' he asked, the tone of his voice suggesting a total lack of doubt.

'I'm sure we are,' Hetty smiled. 'Shall I call you tomorrow?'

'Call me? I thought . . . upstairs?'

'Certainly not. At least not while Megan is in the house.'

'Ah. Yes. You're perfectly right.'

'Tom, I did think we should have left this until tomorrow in case one of us said something to offend the other. Unless I said something to offend you,' she amended. 'When we first met you said something about my relationship with my mother that hurt me. Then, to my dismay, I discovered that Dorothy was of your opinion. That I had allowed myself to be manipulated, controlled by my mother all my life.'

'I'm sure you were as much of a consolation to her as she was a companion to you,' he said softly.

'That's as maybe. I've wasted time, though.'

301

'No experiences are ever wasted.'

'Not if you learn from them. Tom, what I'm trying to say is . . . '

'You've done with being controlled and manipulated. As if I didn't know that already. So what I'm trying to tell you is that I'm smitten to the extent that . . . No, let's be totally honest. I love you, Hetty Loveridge. If we can't progress from there I shall be heart-broken.'

'I doubt . . . No, that's unkind. I think I . . . No, I know that I love you, Tom, but — but it's all too new and strange for me. I'm going to need a lot of — of nurturing over the next few months.'

'Nurturing,' he said reflectively. 'I think I could get to enjoy that.'

'I know I shall,' she said complacently, leaning across and kissing his cheek.

'But you are not about to move in with me?'

Hetty shook her head, though her eyes were moist. 'Do you understand? At fifty-one, my age, I actually feel like a chrysalis. So stupid.' He squeezed her hand. 'Because of the garden, I've met the Beresfords. Do you know, I've never had a proper woman friend before? I think what Mary and I have is something I really, really don't want to lose.'

'Of course you don't. You'll even have a

302

good relationship with Clive now.'

'What makes you say that?'

'Our Clive has done something like this before, you know. He is beginning to miss his wife to the extent he wants to replace her.'

'I had already come to that conclusion.'

'Well . . . So he's accepted that he has to move on? Excellent. Perhaps I'll allow him to keep his teeth.'

'And I'm in a full-time job. A demanding one. One which I like.'

'Which means that we take things slowly. Slowly, slowly catchee monkey?' He grinned.

She was thinking, This monkey is caught already. But it was not something this new Hetty was about to reveal, just yet. 'I think that's just what we shall do,' she agreed.

'I'll make up the couch,' he said. 'Meg'll like to see you here tomorrow. It will give her a sense of security.'

'Fine,' she said. 'Just one pillow for me, please.'

'Oh, no. You'll have my bed. I'll take the couch. As messages go, this one ought to be loud and clear. Up to bed with you, Hetty, my love,' he said, smiling with enormous satisfaction. 'My bed.'

We do hope that you have enjoyed reading this large print book.

Did you know that all of our titles are available for purchase?

We publish a wide range of high quality large print books including:
**Romances, Mysteries, Classics**
**General Fiction**
**Non Fiction and Westerns**

Special interest titles available in large print are:
**The Little Oxford Dictionary**
**Music Book**
**Song Book**
**Hymn Book**
**Service Book**

Also available from us courtesy of Oxford University Press:
**Young Readers' Dictionary**
**(large print edition)**
**Young Readers' Thesaurus**
**(large print edition)**

For further information or a free brochure, please contact us at:
**Ulverscroft Large Print Books Ltd.,**
**The Green, Bradgate Road, Anstey,**
**Leicester, LE7 7FU, England.**
**Tel:** (00 44) **0116 236 4325**
**Fax:** (00 44) **0116 234 0205**

Other titles published by
The House of Ulverscroft:

SEEDS OF DESTRUCTION

A. V. Denham

When Joe set up separate homes with Amanda and Sara he sowed the seeds of destruction. Living with each of them for half the week, he used his deceased Aunt Ethel as an alibi for spending so much time away from his families . . . But the domestic calm becomes threatened, especially when Amanda's son, Simon, meets Harriet, the daughter of Sara . . . As the two women discover Joe's deception, they must sort out their lives. Would it all prove too much for Joe? Could living as one family solve their problems? Can there ever be an acceptable resolution?

# THE STONE BOAT

## A. V. Denham

Three men, Oliver, Philip and Bill, and two women, Ella and Rebecca, decide to walk the Camino, one of the world's great pilgrimages. They all come from very different backgrounds, but are drawn together by their need to move forward. For example, Rebecca is haunted by the sudden death of her children, and Oliver is recovering from a brain tumour. As Santiago de Compostela draws ever nearer, the pilgrims' various reasons for undertaking the strenuous walk are revealed, and the travellers learn a great deal not only about their companions, but also about themselves.